TOLLARD'S PEAK

Glimmer Vale Chronicles #3

MICHAEL KINGSWOOD

CONTENTS

ABOUT THIS BOOK

A man from Raedrick Baletier and Julian Hinderbrook's past turns up on the outskirts of Lydelton, nearly dead from exposure and telling of an injured comrade on the flanks of Tollard's Peak, the tallest mountain in the region.

Despite the harsh winter conditions, the constables form a rescue party and set off to find the injured man.

But the elements are not the only danger that waits to strike down the unwary in the mountains surrounding Glimmer Vale.

Tollard's Peak is the third book of the Glimmer Vale Chronicles, an action-packed trek through a world of valor and magic.

Enjoy the book! After you're done, please come to Michael's website and sign up for his mailing list at www.michaelkingswood.com/newsletter-signup/. Guaranteed to be spam free, he uses it to announce new releases and special promotions for his fans.

MAP OF GLIMMER VALE

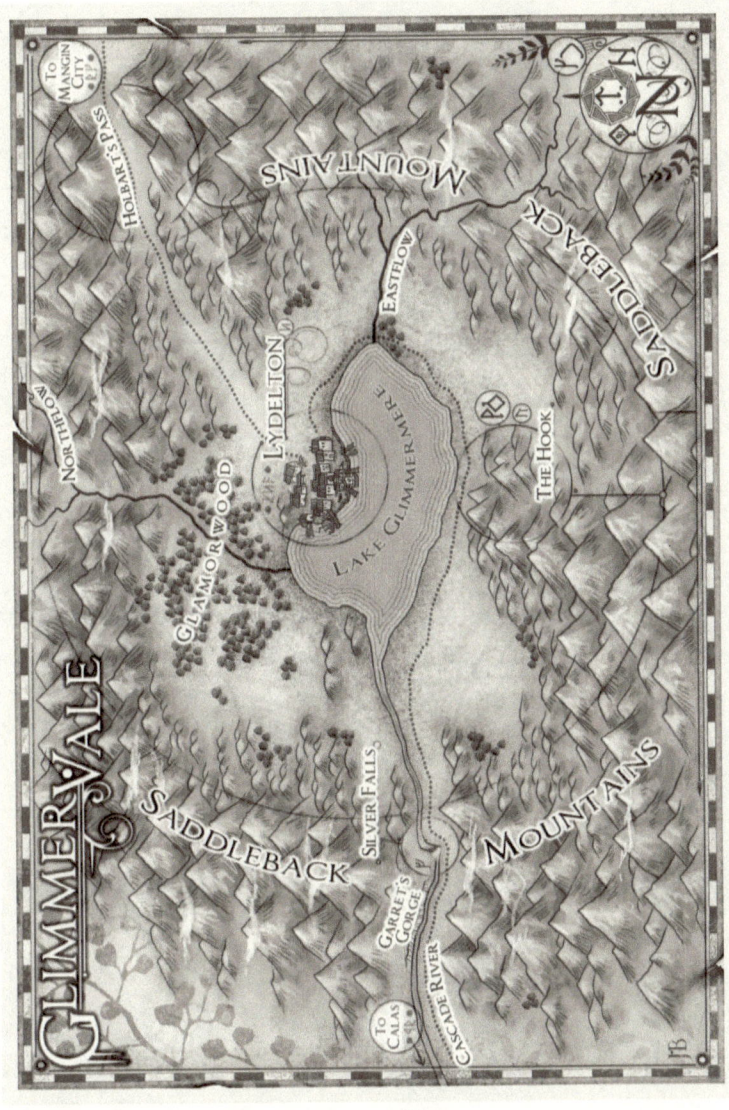

FAMILY COUNSELING

Raedrick Baletier glared at the two men before him and shook his head. This was foolishness, and he expected better, even from them.

They stood, cowed and mostly staring at the floor in front of their feet, in the front room of the Constable's office, a small building that he and Julian Hinderbrook shared as their place of work. The two men were dressed similarly, in bedraggled tunics and breaches; the man on the left in predominately greys and browns, on the right in blue and white. Or at least those had likely been their colors originally. Now their material could better be called stained, it was so covered in grime. They wore matching beards, at least two weeks' worth, and had similar eyes of grey-blue. The rest of their appearances were equally identical: their height, their breadth of shoulder, their lack of a paunch despite their advancing years, their retreating hairlines…

Men such as they, with as many years behind them as they had, should have known better than to get into a brawl in a pub over a woman. Especially over a woman like Yleen Henery, who was young enough to be the daughter of either of the brothers who now looked so abashed in his office.

"Giorg," Raedrick said, and the man on the left gave a little start in recognition of his name. "Pedros." The other man jerked, in the same way that Giorg had a moment before. "What were you two thinking?"

The question sat there in the air between the three of them, unanswered but also somehow unable to depart. It lingered in the air, daring one of the brothers to challenge its primacy over this moment.

Neither did.

Raedrick sighed. "You know I could bring you both up before Judge Telmon."

The pair nodded, in unison.

"Well? Why should I not? You made a mess of Molli's tap room today."

For the first time since Julian, the other of Lydelton's Constables and Raedrick's long-time partner, bundled them into the building, the two brothers glanced at each other. Furtively, as though feeling each other out. But that was a start, at least.

Giorg cleared his throat. "See, it was like this, Constable."

Pedros interrupted. "I've been seeing Yleen for a week now, and he's jealous!" He stretched out a hand toward his brother, his index finger pointing accusingly. Just the way a three year-old would do.

Readrick rolled his eyes and exchanged looks with Julian. The lean man had close-cut brown hair and wore calf-high boots, tight light-brown leggings, a plain white shirt, open at the collar, and green coat that was lined with yellow thread about the cuffs and collar. He leaned against the side of his desk, which lay opposite Raedrick's, his arms crossed over his chest nonchalantly and his lips turned up in a sardonic grin. He winked, and Raedrick had to restrain himself from grinding his teeth in irritation.

He took his irritation out on the twins. Julian may have added the spark that set the tinder ablaze, but they were to blame for stacking the tinder in the first place, so Raedrick did not feel particularly guilty about it.

"I happen to know," he said, in the most biting tone he could muster right then, "that Yleen is all but promised to the young smith's apprentice who works with Fredlin on the east side."

The pair blanched, but said nothing.

Raedrick scowled all the deeper. "You want to tell me why she would be interested in either of you, when she could instead spend her time with him?" Fredlin was just about ready to send his apprentice off on his own. The young man was good-looking - more than good-looking, truth be told - and by all appearances highly skilled and motivated. Small wonder that he was well known as probably the most eligible bachelor in Lydelton.

The brothers traded glances. Silence reigned for a full minute. Then Giorg cleared his throat.

"It's like this, Constable. She smiled and gave me too much change back at lunch."

"She gave me an extra pour of whiskey two nights ago!" Pedros piped up, his tone affronted, almost challenging.

Giorg scowled and drew himself up.

Unbelievable. They were going to fight again, right here in the office. Raedrick glanced past them and saw Julian covering his mouth with his left hand, unsuccessfully trying to hide a broad grin as he clearly attempted to hold back guffaws over the two brothers' cluelessness.

Raedrick rubbed at the bridge of his nose with the thumb and index finger of his left hand, willing an impending headache to stop before he could actually feel it. A headache was the last thing he needed to deal with.

"Gentlemen," he said, using his best parade ground tone, the tone and volume that could cut through the varied sounds and distractions of the grounds to reach his men's ears without difficulty.

They two brothers stopped their glaring and clenching of fists and looked at him, a single eyebrow on each man's forehead rising so similarly that for a second Raedrick wondered whether he was just looking at one man, reflected in a mirror.

He shook his head, focusing in on Giorg, since he had been the instigator. "You do realize that, as a waitress, she had to be nice to her customers, so she can get a larger tip?" He turned his eyes toward Pedros, whose triumphant smile faded immediately when his eyes met Raedrick's. "Or that she might pour more into a customer's cup for the same reason?"

The brothers glowered for a moment, then shook their heads as one.

Raedrick sighed again. "Well, they do." He put on a forced smile and looked the brothers in the eye, one at a time. "Trust me, gentlemen. She is well and truly caught. You need to set your sights elsewhere."

"And if you must fight it out, take it outside," Julian added from behind them. He was still unsuccessful in hiding his disdain for the pair of men.

The brothers looked over their shoulders at Julian and nodded, their expressions rueful.

"Any questions?" Raedrick asked.

Giorg and Pedros looked back at him and shrugged, then shook their heads.

"Good. Now. You're going to pay Molli for the damage you did to her taproom. If I hear from her that you haven't..." He left the threat unstated.

The brothers' faces dropped even further than they had been before.

Raedrick paused for a moment, then continued, "Don't let this happen again or I really will throw you in front of the judge, just to see what he does with you."

The men's eyes widened, going from grudging respect to outright fear in a heartbeat. Poor fellows. They had been in the wrong place at the wrong time, and had gotten the short-end of the intellect stick for decades. But they were not bad people. Not really.

All the same, Raedrick could not have them starting fights in The Oarlock. Even if Molli had not been a friend, The Oarlock was a prominent local business, and it was the Constable's job to maintain the peace.

The twins each made a half-bow and turned away, hurrying out the door as though afraid Raedrick would follow through on his threat right then and there. They hardly glanced at Julian as they left, and his grin faded a bit.

"Well," Julian said, after the door swung shut behind the pair. "How long do you think until we have to deal with them again?" He shook his head and boosted himself off his desk, then sauntered over to the wood stove in the rear corner of the office. Flipping open the little door on its side, he grabbed a piece of seasoned wood from a small stack nearby and shoved it inside the stove. The fire within, which had been on the wane, flared to life again with the soothing popping that always comes from fresh fuel.

"A fortnight at most," Raedrick said. He leaned back in his chair and clasped his hands behind his head, looking up at the ceiling. "Some people have misfortune and trouble follow them, no matter what they try to do to avoid it."

Julian snorted and looked over his shoulder at Raedrick. "There's also people who seek it out, whether they realize it or not." He rubbed his hands in front of the stove for a couple seconds then nodded to himself and moved back over to his desk. He slumped into the chair and kicked one booted foot up. The boot was still soaked with water that a few minutes ago had been snow, and several drops fell onto the blotter that was the primary decoration on Julian's desk.

Readrick nodded. "Granted." He sighed and looked down at his own desk. It was only slightly more cluttered than Julian's. Truth told, their lives as co-Constables of Lydelton were not particularly busy, aside from the routine reports they owed to the Mayor's office. He had seen the offices of big city Constables; they were always covered with files of the cases they were working. Not so for him. His desk held just his blotter, a feather pen and an ink pot, and a small calendar. It was this last that drew Raedrick's attention. He looked at the date, and in particular the date for tomorrow, and sighed again, with more resignation.

"Getting to be that time again," Julian said, his normally cheerful voice growing more somber.

"It is."

Julian cleared his throat. "We don't have to do it, you know."

Raedrick looked askance at him, raising an eyebrow.

"We're in a good place now. There's no need…"

"You know better than that."

Julian frowned, and for a second Raedrick thought he was going to argue more. For what it was worth, Raedrick understood what he was saying, and part of him agreed. Or wanted to, anyway. But it was too soon to set their tradition aside, for many reasons.

Finally, Julian nodded. "All right." He stood and smoothed his tunic then headed toward the door leading to the street. "I'll see you dark and early then," he said. He paused to pull a heavy wool cloak from its peg by the door and settle the garment over his shoulders. Then he stomped his boots into a pair of crampons and flicked the cowl of his cloak up. He looked back at Raedrick, questioningly.

Raedrick returned the nod. "First light. At the end of dock one."

Julian flashed a grin that did not reach his eyes then pulled the door open.

Outside, a bitter wind was blowing, sweeping the snow that had collected along the sides of the street into long drifts and now into their office as well. Julian shivered and pulled his cloak tight around himself. Then, after a long moment, he stepped out into the dimming light of the late winter afternoon. He pulled the door to behind himself as he went, and it shut with the familiar click of the latch catching hold.

Raedrick sat still at his desk. His eyes drifted toward toward the wood stove, where the flickering fire within was just visible through narrow slits that allowed air to flow in. He watched the fire burn and let his thoughts wander. But they never were able to stray far from that horrible day, two years earlier. The day when his world had changed forever, and when he had walked away from any hope of ever having honor again.

Or so he had thought.

Weariness welled up, sparked by the enchanting light of the flames and stoked by his memories, until gradually his eyelids fell and he drifted off into sleep, and the memories of long ago.

❧ 2 ❧

BACK IN THE DAY

Hinderbrook reined in his horse next to Raedrick and made a quick salute, his working uniform stained and dirty over top his mail and his cloak, torn in several places, billowing in the chill wind. The salute was not needed now - in truth, it never had been; Raedrick was no officer - but old habits die hard. Raedrick did not correct him; he just returned the salute.

"What news?"

Hinderbrook rested his hands on his saddle horn and leaned toward him, his normally cheerful eyes somber, troubled. "I think we've lost them. There's been no sign since three days ago, and…"

"You can't know that for certain. They could be just over the next ridge, lying in wait." Tolburt piped up, interrupting the scout's report, and no matter the breach in etiquette. What did such things matter now?

Hinderbrook snorted at the younger man's statement - and Tolburt *was* young; only three months on the front with their unit, and before that he had enlisted at the earliest possible age - and cast a derisive eye his way. "Maybe when you get a little stubble on your chin, you'll figure out how stupid that sounds. I've -"

Raedrick held up a hand and snapped, "Enough."

Hinderbrook fell silent, and Tolburt shut his mouth before speaking the retort that had to have been building on his lips. Both men looked away from each other and focused on Raedrick. Everyone did. All around, the other half-dozen of what remained of Raedrick's squad looked at him intently. Fear, shame, grim determination, but no hope, competed for dominance on their faces.

No hope.

Why should they have any hope? They had done the unthinkable: abandoned their posts, deserted their unit, and in the process killed several of their former comrades. And at least one officer. They could never go back; that would mean the gallows or worse. They could not go home; that would mean the same. Go over to the enemy? That did not even bear consideration. Even if they wouldn't have been killed on sight, why would the enemy welcome them at all? They would certainly never trust them, or allow them to truly join their ranks.

So what could they do? Where could they go, now that they had cast their lot?

Already men had left Raedrick's band. He had not tried to stop them. What right had he to dictate any man's actions now, after what he had led them into? Frankly, he was amazed they all had not left. But men cling to what they know, and there was safety in numbers, especially for men such as they.

He drew a deep breath. "Peace, Tolburt. Let Hinderbrook finish his report."

Hinderbrook nodded quickly, then resumed, Tolburt apparently forgotten. For now. But Raedrick had no doubt Hinderbrook would rib the younger man mercilessly later on. It was all in good fun, of course.

Fun. There was another thing that once had been easy to find, but now seemed lost for all time.

"As I said, no sign. Could be they've called off the hunt."

"Small chance of that," said Kilfer, from Raedrick's right.

Raedrick shot Kilfer a hard look, and the sandy-haired man flashed an apologetic grin. He was right, though. The Army generally did not make it a policy to actively hunt deserters; they tended to show up sooner or later when they got in trouble again - those kinds of men always do - and then they could be taken into custody again easily.

Those kinds of men. His kind of men now.

Raedrick put that thought out of his head, focusing on the immediate problem. It was true that no pursuit was generally conducted, but never before had an entire unit deserted. Raedrick supposed that earned him - and his men - a bit more notoriety and thus more direct attention than the usual discontented riffraff or cowards who generally made up the ranks of deserters.

What he had done, he had done for a reason. A good reason.

It almost helped, telling himself that.

"How far back did you go?" Raedrick asked, turning his attention back to Hinderbrook.

Hinderbrook shrugged. "About a half-day's ride."

Raedrick frowned, considering.

"Maybe he's right." Shermyn murmured.

"Could be," Raedrick replied. He turned to Laremy. "Get the map."

Laremy nodded and opened his saddlebag. He rifled around in there for a few seconds, then pulled out a rolled up piece of parchment, which he brought over to Raedrick and unrolled onto a moderate-sized rock that protruded from the ground.

Raedrick squatted down, frowning at the map. It was no great piece of cartography; a squad leader does not rate those. Hand drawn, copied from the real maps kept by the general's staff, it only showed the major features of the area immediately around the current area of operations. In this case, it extended only as far east as Ysoldor, the Kingdom's western-most outpost, though it could hardly be said to reside within the Kingdom's borders at all. The next city worthy of the title that the Kingdom claimed, and that the Kingdom truly held dominion over, lay a good two months' ride further east.

The rest of the map's features were less familiar. The great sea to the south, the mountains to the north, and the enemy's strongholds and cities to the west and northeast. There were many places they could go, and a few that may offer the promise of refuge; they might be able to hire on to a ship at one of the ports along the sea and sail to some distant land where no one would know or care about what they had done.

All the same, Raedrick's eyes kept drifting back to Ysoldor and beyond, to the east. Toward home.

But going that direction was madness.

"I think you're right, Kilfer," Raedrick said, earning a quirked eyebrow in response. He managed a wry grin. "The ships are our best bet." He traced a line from the little X where Larmey had marked his best approximation of their current position to the nearest port city, a place called Qoramyr. "We ought to be able to make it in a week or less, if we ride hard."

Kilfer smiled, the first genuine smile Raedrick had seen on his face in more days than he wanted to count.

"Thought you'd never see the light."

Raedrick shrugged. "I wanted to be sure before…" He left the rest of the thought go unstated.

All around, his men nodded slowly, their faces solemn. Only Kilfer seemed to relish the notion of taking the ships. For the rest, taking that route would be as it was for Raedrick: a trip with no return, their homes forever lost to them. As long as they remained on the mainland, there was at least the slight hope that perhaps they could return someday. But if they left…

Raedrick sighed and stood from his crouch, pulling his vest down over his hips better. No sense dwelling on what could not be. They needed to get going if they had any hope of getting there without being caught.

"Saddle up,"

His men dispersed to their mounts. Within five minutes, they were gone, leaving no trace behind except tracks in the turf.

As they rode away, Raedrick looked back at the little hillock that had been his, and his men's, home for the last several days. Professional pride over his people's ability to remove all sign of their presence fell beneath a deep and abiding sadness. Would they ever again have a place to call home, where they could actually set down roots?

In the lands beyond the sea. If there was any hope at all, it lay there.

He straightened in his saddle and faced forward, then spurred his horse to greater speed, not daring to allow himself to believe in that hope, beckoning like a will o' the wisp in the dark.

Ten minutes later, even that tiny shred of hope withered and died.

Raedrick and his men rounded a fair-sized hill - they road around its base instead of riding over it, to avoid standing out to any spying eyes - and found themselves face to face with a platoon of the Kingdom's Elite Guards.

Fifty soldiers in mail and plate, their armor gleaming in the afternoon sunlight, their banners whipping gently in the breeze, sat mounted in a semicircle blocking the path ahead and avenues of escape to the sides.

Raedrick reined in, his heart in his throat, before the gruff voice of the Guards' commander could order it. This the worst of all possible things that could have happened. The Guards, lying in wait for them. How?

He jerked on his reins, to turn his horse and gallop back the way they came, but no sooner did he get the animal's head around than he saw a second platoon fanning out behind them, cutting off any retreat.

Laremy drew his sword. "We can cut through." He voice trembled slightly, the only hint of nervousness in his demeanor; coming from him, that indicated absolute terror.

Raedrick reached for his saber. It was hopeless, but better to go out fighting, as a free man, than to await the end in the prison at Divisional Headquarters.

Cold steel, honed to a razor's edge, came to rest upon his throat, stopping him. Raedrick turned his head, ever so slowly, to see his attacker, and all hope, all will to fight or even try any more, left him.

Tolburt swallowed, beads of sweat forming on his brow quickly, despite the afternoon's relative coolness. What he did terrified the young man, but he did not lower the blade, nor did it tremble at all in his hand.

"I'm sorry, Corporal," Tolburt said.

And then the Guards moved in.

✦ 3 ✦

MAKING THE ROUNDS

Raedrick jerked awake. For a moment, he was unsure where he was. Then his mind absorbed his surroundings: the long room with a plain desk opposite the one he sat behind. The rack of swords behind the other desk and the wood stove in the corner to its right. The cabinet of files next to a door made of steel bars that led further back into the building.

His office.

Embarrassment flooded through him. He had not realized he fell asleep. It must have been the late night last night, out with Molli and Lani, Molli's daughter and partner in the running of the Oarlock, and Raedrick's...he was not sure what to call their relationship. More than friendship certainly. But beyond that... He shook his head. The remaining fatigue from their fun combined with the fire and the memories coming back must have lulled him. And in the middle of the afternoon, as well. That simply would not do.

Raedrick glanced at the window.

Dim light still shown from outside; he must not have slept very long, thank goodness. There was still work to be done today, preparations for tomorrow morning. He could understand Julian's reluctance, his desire to move on, put the past aside. But

15

Raedrick still felt the need to pay homage. Maybe someday it would be different, but not now.

He shook his head with a snort and pushed himself to his feet. That was enough grousing. He ought to make one last sweep of the town before it got dark.

Raedrick took a moment to buckle on his sword belt, strap on his crampons, and slip on his cloak, thick black wool that was lined in some sort of softer fabric that prevented the itching that he always hated about wool. Then he tugged on his gloves and slipped out the door.

The wind, if anything, was even worse than it had been before. He had to brace himself against its force to make headway toward Main Street, and his cloak constantly threatened to flap open, exposing him to winter's icy embrace. He hunched over, resigning himself to making slow progress and questioning the wisdom of going back outside again.

But he had a job to do.

Main Street's paving stones presented a different challenge than the dirt - well, dirt below the layers of snow and ice that had accumulated over the winter - of the side street that housed the Constable's office building. The fishing guild, and others whose normal jobs offered little in the way of employment during the winter months, did a better job of keeping the stones clear of snow than the dirt. But the stones also made for a more ready surface for ice to cling to. Thus, it was always a challenge walking anywhere. Very early in this, their first winter in Lydelton, Readrick and Julian had learned the value of strapping crampons onto their boots, even in town.

Raedrick turned east and began walking. The street was empty of people; everyone else had the sense to stay inside where it was warm.

Why don't you?

Raedrick smirked at his own foolishness, then pressed on to the edge of town, where Main Street ended and turned into the dirt road that stretched southeast from Lydelton along the shore of Lake Glimmermere to the Eastflow.

He always started on the east edge of town and moved west during his sweeps. No particular reason why, except maybe that was the direction Isenholf's band of brigands had come from, all those months ago when Raedrick and Julian had helped defend the town from them.

He wondered how Isenholf had met his end. When he went to the gallows in Mangan City, had he taken it with pride and dignity, or had he begged and pleaded? Theobald had never been the bravest of men in battle; Raedrick could not recall any instance during their time in the Army together that he had led the van. But he was skilled - very skilled - and seemed to relish a fight when it was one-on-one. The ghost of remembered pain in Raedrick's leg recalled the wound he had taken during the final fight with Isenholf, and he grimaced for a moment before bringing his thoughts back to the present.

A sound carried over the howling wind, making Raedrick stop in his tracks. It was a person's voice, raised in a shout, but he could not make out the words. He turned a circle where he stood, peering out into the storm.

From the west, a man was laboring through the blowing snow, hurrying in Raedrick's direction. The figure shouted, and Raedrick could just make out the word this time.

"Constable!"

Raedrick hurried toward the approaching man, his mind whirling through the possibilities that could bring this man chasing after him in these conditions. None of them were good. He met the man a minute or so later, and he saw it was Tom, one of the fishing men who worked for the town during the winter months.

Tom was older, well past his prime. On the boats, he was the master navigator. His joints would not let him haul in the nets the way he used to, but he still had a fine eye and he knew the shoals and hazards of the Lake better than anyone, or so Horace, the head of the local fishing guild, had told Raedrick. Raedrick did not know Tom all that well; the thing that stood out most was the older man had scraggly gray hair that shot out in all directions when his head was uncovered. Now, he was bundled up for the cold in a heavy coat, gloves, hat, and boots. Only his face, and his long, bulbous nose, was exposed to the elements. Right then, Raedrick considered that Tom was quite a bit smarter than he was.

"What is it, Tom?"

The older man leaned forward, placing his hands on his knees and panting for a few moments before answering. "They need you at the Healers Circle," he said after he had regained his breath.

Uh-oh. "Did they say what the problem is?"

Tom shook his head. "Just to come get you."

That really did not sound good.

"Alright, I'm on my way. Please find Julian, and ask him to join me. He's probably at The Oarlock."

Tom's face lit up at the mention of the Inn's name. No doubt he was looking forward to getting indoors and having a pint or two. For that matter, Raedrick could use some of that as well.

"Can do, Constable," Tom said. Then he turned and shambled off through the snow.

The Healers Circle in Lydelton occupied a small building on the north side of town, one block north of Main Street and two blocks west of Raedrick's and Julian's office building. Like all Healers Circles across the Kingdom, it was of simple construction, sturdy and functional, with no excesses to speak of. The front of the building was dominated, as most buildings in Lydelton were, by a porch that ran the building's width, complete with hitching post. A simple sign announcing the Healers Circle's ownership of the building hung over the double-doors leading within, and was the only nod to the need for advertisement at all.

Not that there really was any need for the Healers Circle to advertise. Their guild was known far and wide: men and women who willingly gave aid to whomever needed it, regardless of circumstance and of the patient's ability to pay. For the Guildsmen of the Healers Circle, treating illness and injury was all, everything else was secondary.

Or at least that's what they told the world. Raedrick had often wondered how they got the funding to go about their mission without charging anything beyond a request for whatever donation a person felt reasonable and responsible to give. He had donated to them a number of times himself, though he had never had occasion to require more than simple services. But the little he gave could not have stretched far. He could not fathom how the guild stayed afloat if that was the only way they gained income.

Which was neither here nor there for this afternoon's purposes.

Raedrick rapped firmly on the entrance doors, then stepped back to wait. One did not burst into the Healers Circle, after all; there was an etiquette to it that had to be obeyed, if one wished to remain in their good favor. Of course, they would still treat you, even if you fell out of favor with them, so a cynical man might wonder what was the point? Raedrick prided himself on not being cynical.

Several minutes passed, and the cold, held at bay before by the energy he used to walk here, quickly soaked through his heavy cloak and into his flesh. By the time the door latch clicked open, he had begun to shiver. Quite a bit. This was not shaping up as a good evening to be out and about.

The door opened and an elderly man of average height - though he once had been tall, judging by the stoop of his shoulders - dressed in the white and yellow robes of the Healers Circle guildsmen looked him up and down for a second.

"Ah, Constable," said the man, as he flashed a warm smile

Raedrick's way. "Good of you to come." He pulled the door open fully and waved for Raedrick to enter.

Moving quickly, and grateful to get into the warmth, Raedrick stepped inside and cleared the way so the guildsman could shut the door behind him. "My pleasure, Master Sebastini." Raedrick glanced around the familiar entryway and did not see anything awry. The armchairs lining the far wall, where people with conditions that were non-emergency in nature could sit while awaiting the guildsmen, were as they always had been. The tapestries depicting guildsmen treating patients in all manner of settings still hung, intact, on the walls. The usual subtle scent of cleanness lingered in the air. No, nothing appeared out of the ordinary at all. "What seems to be the trouble?"

Sebastini pursed his lips and gestured for Raedrick to follow, then set off through the narrow doorway leading back into the treatment rooms and guild spaces in the rear of the building. "Not trouble, as such. But I thought you ought to know we have a new patient."

That was hardly unusual. "Oh?"

Sebastini nodded, not looking back at him. "One of Horace's men found him curled up on the ice of the lake, beside one of the docks. They brought him here not a half hour ago."

Raedrick blinked. "He was on the ice?"

It was hardly unusual for people to go out on the lake in the wintertime. The ice was, by now, more than thick enough to support them, and they found all manner of amusements on its frozen surface. Raedrick almost killed himself the first time Lani introduced him to those things she called skates, and he had not attempted it a second time. But there were many in Lydelton who reveled in them. And some of Horace's fishing men would actually cut holes in the ice to fish through. It did not make for a large catch by any measure, but they seemed to enjoy it.

But no one would go out on the lake in conditions like existed today. That was just asking for trouble at best, tragedy at worst.

The old man stopped in front of a closed door and gave

Raedrick a wry look. "He is not a local or I would chalk it up to a young man behaving foolishly on a stormy day." He drew himself up and seemed to undergo a transformation. The stooped, kindly man suddenly took on an air of calm professionalism, and for a second it was like Raedrick was looking at a different man. "We are keeping the room quite warm, to ease the chill from his bones." He lifted an eyebrow.

Raedrick nodded acknowledgment, and Sebastini unlatched the door and led in him side.

Quite warm was not the word for it. The room was very nearly stifling, like a hayloft on a hot summer day. But then, Raedrick had to admit that a spring afternoon would likely feel stifling to him right that moment, having come so quickly out of the bitterly cold evening.

The room within was not large, and it was nearly filled with furniture and the accoutrements of the guildsmen's trade. The heat came from a brazier full of hot coals in the far corner. Light smoke wafted from the brazier, bringing the scent of some exotic incense Raedrick did not recognize. Shelves full of jars containing medicines of some sort or other lined the wall to Raedrick's right and a bureau rested against the wall to his left. A narrow bed stood in the center of the room. A thin, tall man with scraggly black hair and a matching beard lay sprawled unconscious on the bed, covered head to toe in blankets.

Beside him, on a small wooden stool, sat a younger man in guildsmen's robes. Dark skinned, with black hair that reached to his shoulders and eyes that were closer to yellow than brown, Sebastini's apprentice - or whatever the guildsmen called their underlings - nodded and flashed a quick smile of greeting. "Constable."

"How goes our patient, Willam?" Sebastini said, closing the door behind them.

Willam shrugged, then bent over to where a bucket lay on the ground. He reached into the bucket and pulled out a water-logged rag. Wringing out the majority of the water, he dabbed at the unconscious man's forehead gently before replying. "Better, Master," he said. "He mumbled something a few minutes ago, but I could not make it out."

Sebastini nodded. "That is a good sign."

Raedrick stepped to the bedside, peering down at the sick man. He was pale, extremely pale, and his cheekbones protruded from his skin as though he had not had a good meal in a while.

Willam dabbed at the man's forehead again, and he wriggled slightly, turning his head away from the apprentice's ministrations. The man's profile stood out for a moment in the glow from the brazier, and Raedrick frowned. There was something familiar about him.

"What is his temperature now?" Sebastini asked.

Willam frowned and consulted a small notepad. "Twenty-six, as of five minutes ago."

Sebastini gave a satisfied nod and pulled a small bottle down from one of the shelves. "It should be safe to try to wake him now," he took a dropper out and, unscrewing the bottle, withdrew a small small amount of green-blue fluid. Then he replaced the bottle's top and returned it to the shelf, and came over to stand next to Raedrick, "so the Constable can do his job."

"Is that a good…"

The patient let out a little groan and turned his head again. His eyes cracked open slightly.

Sebastini chuckled and glanced at Raedrick with a little shrug of his shoulders. "No need after all, hmm?"

The patient squirmed weakly beneath the covers and blinked his eyes several times. He tried to say something, but all that came out was a croak.

"Easy, son," Sebastini said. "You've had a hard afternoon." He looked up at his apprentice. "Water."

Willam already had things in hand. He held a small cup to the man's lips. He drank, sparingly at first but then with greater gusto, grabbing the cup with both hands. He finished with a sigh and held the cup out to Willam, who went to refill it from a decanter on the shelf nearby.

"Who are you?" Raedrick said, leaning a bit closer.

The man turned bleary gray-green eyes toward him, and Raedrick took a half-step backwards in shock. He knew those eyes.

The patient's eyes widened and his expression changed from confusion to shock to hope to fear to resignation in under a second. He spoke, barely loudly enough to hear, his voice trembling. "Corporal... Is it really you?"

The voice made the patient's identity a certainty, though Raedrick had never thought to see him alive again.

It was Tolburt.

4

STRANDED

"Throw him out into the snow."

At first, Raedrick thought certain Julian was not being serious. Then he saw the fire in his friend's eyes, the scowl that spoke of an anger beyond rage, and he realized Julian would do exactly that, if Raedrick let him.

They stood in the entrance hall of the Healers Circle, where Raedrick and Master Sebastini had retreated after Tolburt drifted off to sleep again. He had not said much more, being only awake for a few moments, and left Raedrick with more questions than answers about what he was doing there. Julian had arrived only a few minutes later and Raedrick briefed him on the situation.

Sebastini moved before Raedrick could respond to Julian's reaction, interposing himself between Julian and the doorway leading back to the patient rooms and placing his hands on his hips in a manner that managed to look imposing, despite his stoop. "You will do no such thing, Constable. He is our patient, and under the protection of the guild. If you think you can force it..." He shook his head, giving Julian a level look that spoke of a willingness to use whatever force necessary.

Julian looked incredulously at Sebastini for a moment. Their eyes met, and Julian's widened ever so slightly. Then he turned away, muttering softly to himself. Raedrick could not make out the words, but his disgusted tone was plain enough.

"I understand how you feel, Julian," Raedrick said, "but..."

Julian whirled on him, jabbing a finger into the air between them. "Damn right you understand. He sold us out. And now we're offering him aid." He snorted. Loudly.

Raedrick could only nod in agreement. What else was there to say?

"*You* are not, young man," Sebatini said. "We are." He glanced between Julian and Raedrick for a second, clearly curious about their history with Tolburt. Then he shrugged slightly. "If you will excuse me." He did not wait for them to respond, but turned and departed the entrance hall.

No doubt he was going back to help Willam. And Tolburt.

Silence reigned for a full minute, Julian, from all appearances fuming quietly to himself while Raedrick tried not to follow suit.

Finally, Julian broke the silence. "What the hell is he doing here?"

Raedrick shook his head. "No idea. He only woke up for those couple of minutes."

"Well there has to be..."

He broke off as Willam walked into the room. The young apprentice nodded to them politely by way of greeting. "He is awake again, and asking for you."

Raedrick shared a brief look with Julian. He looked strangely reluctant; Raedrick suddenly felt similarly. But whatever his feelings about the return of their erstwhile comrade...betrayer... whatever, he had a job to do. So he squared his shoulders and followed Willam back into the treatment room.

Tolburt was fully awake when they returned to the room, and halfway sitting up supported by two or three pillows stacked behind his back. He clutched a large mug - almost a bowl - that wafted steam almost like a freshly drawn bath in the depths of winter, and sipped from it every other second or so. He was talking with Sebastini when they walked in, but stopped mid-word when he saw Raedrick. When Julian followed him into the room, Tolburt's mouth dropped wide open.

"Nice to see you too," Julian quipped, his tone dripping acid. So much for being polite and professional.

Tolburt winced slightly at the tone and looked away, toward the wall to Raedrick's left.

Raedrick gave Julian a hard look, but he either did not notice it or pretended not to. Rolling his eyes slightly, Raedrick turned his attention fully onto Tolburt. "You want to tell us how you came to be on our lake today, Tolburt?"

Tolburt continued staring at nothing for a few seconds. Then he shook himself and tore his eyes away, looking instead at Raedrick. Something almost like relief showed on his face, as though he had been worried to be alone with Julian. Then, just as quickly that look faded, replaced by a somber expression. He sipped at his mug and was silent for a moment before he swallowed.

"Where to start?" He paused and sipped his mug again. "My friend and I found an old map that pointed to the mountains north of here." He flashed an almost apologetic smile as he added, "Supposedly it leads to a hidden cache of money and equipment." He drew a deep breath. "A *lot* of money."

Raedrick exchanged a look with Julian. Skeptical did not begin to describe his expression.

"I see," Raedrick said. "Where did this map come from?"

Tolburt shrugged. He paused for a moment, then said, "We thought about waiting until spring, but other people were looking for this place too. And besides, it hadn't gotten that cold yet…"

"Down in the lowlands, it hadn't," Julian interjected. "Up here is a different matter."

Tolburt nodded, a rueful smile flitting across his features for a second. "Should have thought of that." He sipped at the mug again. "But by the time we got up here, it would have been stupid to go back. And besides, we had it under control."

"Until..." Raedrick prompted.

"Until this storm came in. It caught us in the open, and we couldn't see where we were going. Stefan fell into a ditch and broke his leg." He shivered involuntarily, almost spilling his drink, whatever it was. "We'd seen the lights of the town, down by the lake. I got him to as good a shelter as I could, got a fire going and enough wood to see him for a while, then left to get help." He lowered his eyes. "Guess I got turned around in the storm. I didn't even realize I was on the ice at first. Then it seemed like a good idea to stay, because it was flat. After that..." He shook his head. "I don't remember much after that."

"Crap," Raedrick said to himself, softly. Sebastini glanced at him, an eyebrow quirking upward, and Raedrick fought through a momentary surprise that the older man had heard him. He was quite a bit more capable than he appeared at first glance. Or maybe the weak, hunched look was just an act, to throw people off balance.

That thought made Raedrick roll his eyes, at his own foolishness. He was just trying to not think about what he had to consider here. He cleared his throat. "Do you know where... Stefan?" Tolburt nodded. "Where Stefan is now? Can you draw us a map?"

Tolburt looked up, surprise on his face and a faint hope in his eyes. He nodded again. "I think so." He drew a deep breath. "Thank you, Corporal. You've no idea what..."

"*Constable*," Julian said firmly, but he was looking at Raedrick questioningly, and apparently not liking what he was seeing. More softly, he said, "Can I talk to you, Rae?"

Raedrick nodded quickly. "Draw your map, Tolburt." Then he gestured for Julian to lead the way back out of the room.

"Tell me you're not really thinking about doing this?" Julian demanded. They were back in the entrance hall, and he looked fit to be tied.

"Stefan is stranded out there. Injured. He could die without help." That was all there was to it.

Julian shook his head. "Well you could die trying to get to him. Have you *seen* the weather outside?" He waved at the double-doors leading outside, and just then the wind decided to howl menacingly through the cracks around their edges.

Convenient.

Raedrick suppressed a shiver as he contemplated the bitter cold, about to become all that much worse once full dark settled in, outside. "We can't just leave him out there."

"Bollocks. We don't owe Tolburt a damn thing, and you know it. You know he didn't tell you the whole truth in there. He's the kind of guy…"

Raedrick narrowed his eyes, sudden anger welling up within him. "That what?" he said, softly, coldly. "The kind of guy that what?"

Julian met his gaze for a long moment, then looked away, still scowling but some of the heat gone from his gaze.

"Whatever he is now, he became that because of us." Raedrick looked back down the hallway toward the treatment rooms. "Because of *me*," he amended, more softly.

Julian snorted. Loudly and with gusto. "You know better than that, Rae."

He thought he did. But… Maybe it was the fact that their anniversary was coming up tomorrow. Last year it was the same thing. Guilt, the weight of the burden he bore for the lives of his men. His men whom he had led into treason. They had paid the price, while he escaped and, indeed, had prospered here.

It should have been he who paid, and they who survived.

But even if guilt were not driving him, the fact remained that he could not in good conscience leave a man to freeze to death out there. Not if there was a chance they could rescue him.

Raedrick drew a deep breath in through his nose and slowly exhaled through his mouth. Then did it again. And again. Slowly, he calmed himself, let the guilt and doubt fade into focus. He knew what he had to do.

"You don't have to come, Julian," he said. "One of us should stay and keep an eye on things around town."

There was a long pause, and then Julian said, "I'm not going to convince you, am I?"

Raedrick shook his head, still looking back toward the treatment room.

"Bugger me."

5

PREPARATIONS

The door closed behind Julian, leaving Raedrick to ponder the situation alone for several minutes before Sebastini came back out of the treatment room.

Julian was right. This was likely going to be a futile effort, and could very well lead only to sorrow. But there was no choice. Had Tolburt not been involved, it would not even be a question whether they would send aid to a person stranded up in the mountains. So forget about Tolburt. It was not about him. Not really.

"You are going after this Stefan."

Sebastini did not pose it as a question, but Raedrick nodded in response anyway.

The elderly guildsman pursed his lips for a moment, then nodded to himself. "I shall accompany you." He held a piece of parchment out to Raedrick.

He did not notice for a second, so shocked he was by Sebastini's announcement. He was...what? No, that would not do. Raedrick shook his head vehemently. "That's not a good idea, Master Sebastini. It's going to be a difficult climb, and you..."

"I have more time in these mountains than you, young man. I can handle myself."

Raedrick opened his mouth again, to protest, but Sebastini cut him off with a raised hand.

"This fellow is injured and, by the time we find him, will be suffering from exposure. If you are to have any chance of getting him down the mountain alive, you will need my skills." He smiled, his eyes twinkling. "And besides, I've been cooped up in here for far too long. Willam will welcome my absence."

"I really think you should stay here. Send Willam with us. He can…"

Sebastini shook his head. "Willam is a capable young man, but he does not yet have the skills for a case such as this."

Raedrick looked him steadily in the eye and saw only stubborn resolve. There would be no talking him out of it.

Crap.

"Is that the map?"

Sebastini nodded and held it out to him again. Raedrick examined it by the light of one of the room's wall-lamps. It was rough. Very rough.

"I believe the large mountain referenced there is Tollard's Peak," Sebastini said.

Raedrick frowned, considering the drawing. It could be.

"Povol Gerberson climbed Tollard's Peak a year and a half ago, you know."

Raedrick blinked, surprised. He looked at Sebastini for confirmation, and the old man nodded affirmative.

"But…I thought they said it could not *be* climbed."

Sebastini chuckled. "Not by anyone but Povol. I suggest you ask him to be our guide. There is no one better in the Vale."

Raedrick blinked again.

"You *were* planning to bring a guide? Or did you magically gain knowledge of the mountains when I wasn't looking?"

Sebastini was just boxing him in on all sides. The clever old fox. Despite himself, Raedrick laughed. He nodded acquiescence.

"Good." Sebastini sounded satisfied. "We leave at first light then?"

"I was thinking immediately."

The guildsman pursed his lips, then shook his head. "It will make no difference to Stefan if we take a few more hours to get to him. But if we perish because we went blundering around in the dark, it will make quite a large difference indeed."

Again, he had a good point. Raedrick nodded. "First light then."

"I look forward to it."

Raedrick found Povol without too much difficulty. He presumed the outdoorsman would be at Holb's Tavern; for whatever reason, people of his ilk seemed to prefer it, while the fishing men and craftsmen kept to The Oarlock.

Holb, towering and bulky as ever and dressed in simple wool clothing beneath a white apron, scowled at him when Raedrick pushed aside the canvas flap that served as the entrance to his tavern. For whatever reason, he rubbed the tavern keeper wrong; Holb had actually thrown him out of the place the first time he ventured inside. Since then, relations between them had improved, but only marginally.

All the same, Raedrick had no desire to chitchat with him any longer than necessary. "Have you seen Povol?"

Holb grunted and nodded toward the corner to his left, where the canvas pavilion that enclosed the sitting area met the side of the building housing the bar. A half-dozen roughly dressed men crowded around a small table there, all talking over each other in between drinks from their tankards. They made a small cacophony that, for all its volume, seemed good-natured enough.

Raedrick nodded thanks to Holb and meandered over toward the table. As he went, he scanned the rest of the sitting area and shook his head. He could not understand how Holb or his customers preferred this setup to a properly constructed building. The only part of the tavern that had a real wall was the bar, and it was literally a hole cut into the side of a building. Braziers scattered around kept the place warm enough, but the wind whipping around made the canvas of the pavilion flap annoyingly, and every now and then a particularly forceful gust would force itself within, overcoming the braziers with a blast of cold. The place was nice enough in the summer, short as that was, but now, in the depths of winter?

The world accommodates all kinds.

That was true enough, he supposed.

One member of the boisterous group, sitting with his back to the canvas wall, noticed Raedrick's approach and raised his tankard in a small salute. Raedrick did not recognize him: a thin, almost wiry man of about Raedrick's age with short blond hair and grey eyes who wore a green coat over an off-white shirt.

"Constable," the blond man said by way of greeting, his voice cutting through his fellows' conversation easily. All eyes at the table turned toward Raedrick, and the men made quick nods of greeting. "Why do we get the pleasure of your company tonight?"

Raedrick chuckled softly at the man's tone, light and slightly teasing, then returned the nod. "Gentlemen," he said. "Just need to talk with Povol for a moment."

He had only met Povol once, a few months back, but he picked the mountaineer out from his fellows easily enough. He sat to Raedrick's right and wore clothing of nondescript homespun wool; good for braving the elements but hardly the height of fashion. He was bald, short and stocky, with powerfully muscled arms and legs: they say he could take a man lying on the ground and lift him up over his head without assistance. Of course, *they* say lots of things that most times do not end up being true.

Povol's eyebrow rose when Raedrick named him and he took a quick swig from his tankard. "I didn't do it. It wasn't me." He grinned, showing a gap in his front upper teeth where he had lost one. "You can't prove it."

The other men around the table laughed uproariously, making

Raedrick feel certain he was missing something in this conversation.

But that was not important right then.

"I need your help, Povol. There's an injured man up near Tollard's Peak, and we're sending out an expedition in the morning to bring him to safety."

The smiles around the table faded immediately, the outdoorsmen's expressions becoming grim. Povol's eyes narrowed.

"What kind of a fool goes up there on a day like this?"

Raedrick related Tolburt's story and handed Povol the map. The mountaineer frowned as he began the telling. By the time he reached the end, Povol's frown had become a full-on scowl.

"Bloody idiots." He peered at the map for a long time, his scowl only getting worse. "Yeah that's Tollard's Peak all right. And the canyon to the northeast." He shook his head and raised his eyes - they were a deep shade of green, and why Raedrick should notice that right then was beyond him - to meet Raedrick's. He did not look hopeful. "I know that area well, but there's not enough here to go on. This guy could be anywhere in a ten square mile area, from what this shows."

A lump of cold developed in Raedrick's belly. Fear? Why was he afraid over this man he had never met? But he knew the answer to that question before he asked it of himself.

"Nevertheless, we're heading out tomorrow at first light. I would like to have you along to keep the rest of us out of trouble." Raedrick flashed a grin and put on a more cheerful tone. "Think of it as your good turn for the year."

Povol snorted. Loudly. "Last good turn I did almost cost me a finger." He looked intently at Raedrick, and the Constable could see the wheels turning as Povol thought it through. Finally, Povol nodded. "Fine. But I want double my normal rates." He grinned wolfishly. "Compensation for the lateness of the request and the unpleasant weather."

Raedrick blinked. He had not anticipated that Povol might demand payment. He and Julian did not have much of an operating budget. In point of fact, they did not really have a budget at all. City Hall paid them and paid for the ladies who kept up their office building. But aside from that… They had not really needed much in the way of money at all since they took over the job. What would the Mayor say about this outlay?

It did not matter. Stefan needed help, and Raedrick was going to deliver. He could worry about the financial aspects later.

"Agreed," he said, and held out his hand to Povol.

Povol's grin broadened and he took Raedrick's hand in a powerful grip. "First light then. Meet up at my place. Me and my dogs'll be ready."

Raedrick nodded, then turned and left the tavern. It was going to be a long day tomorrow and he needed to get some rest. It did not take long, after he reached his flat, for sleep to come, and with it, memories.

6

ENTRAPPED

The squad, tied hand and foot into their saddles, rode single-file under the direction of their captors, toward the divisional headquarters, Raedrick had no doubt. He rode at the rear of the column, and could only see the back of the man in front of him - Laremy - and the guards who rode on either side of them.

So this was it. This was what came from doing the right thing, refusing an unconscionable order, being true to his conscience. In spite of his best efforts, he had, in fact, only led his men to the gallows.

Had he been alone, Raedrick thought certain he would break down in tears at the injustice of it all.

But he was not alone. Even if they were only going to their graves, his men looked to him and he had to be strong, to remain true to principle. That was what they needed. Or maybe it was what *he* needed. Regardless, it was all he could allow himself to do. So he rode with his head high, eyes up and not lowered like one who has been defeated.

Of course no one noticed. His men were just focused on the road ahead, and the guards. For their part, the guards simply diverted themselves with jokes at one another's, or more often at the prisoners', expense. Then, as the afternoon wore on, they became more focused on picking out a good place to pitch camp for the night.

And so it was that the troop came to a halt with Raedrick riding like a king, at least in his own mind, but being ignored altogether. Oh well, it was the thought that counted.

For the prisoners, camp was simple. Their bonds were released to allow them to dismount, one at a time, but then quickly re-tied. And then they were tied again, onto a long picket-line similar to what the men would have done with the horses. Once they were secure, their captors set two men to guarding them while the rest erected the remainder of the camp.

Tents. Lots of tents. But not one of them for Raedrick or his men. At least they were allowed dinner. A meager dinner, far less than their captors ate, but also more than they had been able to indulge in during their time on the run. But when sentries were set and the rest of the soldiers bedded down for the night - in their tents - Raedrick and his men were left to ride out the night under the stars, along with their pair of guards.

Raedrick did not mind so much, at first. Most nights since they deserted he and his men had not had shelter for the night. But not long after sunset, clouds rolled in and with them, rain. A slow but steady rain that seemed at first nothing to complain about, but then sooner than he thought possible left him soaked and shivering.

All around him, his men tossed and turned, complaining in muffled tones but unable to get to sleep. Surely their anxiety about what lay ahead contributed to that, and the rain only made it worse. But they were hardened soldiers, and soldiers caught sleep whenever the opportunity arose. Sleep was a weapon.

Of course, knowing death was a possibility was much

different than knowing it was certain. Hard to calm yourself down when facing that.

"What are we going to do, Corporal?"

The whispered words came from Raedrick's left. He could not see the man's face, but he knew the voice. Tolburt.

What was Tolburt doing here with them?

"Shut up, you traitor." That was Laremy, Raedrick was sure.

Tolburt's snorted response spoke volumes.

"Enough," Raedirck said, putting on his best command tone of voice. Or as best as he could while keeping it low enough to not alert the guards. Around him, men who were tossing and muttering went silent, and Raedrick felt a sense of anticipation from them. As if somehow he had a plan, and once he expressed it they would get out of this and everything would be ok.

If only.

Raedrick drew a breath, pondering what to say. "I don't know," he said, finally. It was the truth, but he hated it as soon as he said it. He could feel his men deflating all around him. But what was he supposed to do, lie to them? He had no idea how they were going to get out of this, if it was even possible.

Better to not give them false hope.

"You rat bastard!" The words came from further to Raedrick's left and were spoken with such fury, such fiery hatred, that Raedrick could not at first tell who had spoken them.

Tolburt cried out suddenly, surprise and pain combining to make his scream high-pitched like a woman's. He screamed again, more shrilly - Raedrick would not have thought that was possible.

What was going on?

Down the picket line, a torch bobbed closer; the guards were coming.

"Get off of me!" Tolburt finally managed to shout coherently, and there was the sound of men thrashing around in the dark.

"Here now, what's this? Stop it, you!" The guards had arrived, and by the light of the torch, Raedrick could see Tolburt and Hinderbrook engaged in a strange sort of wrestling, if it could be called wrestling with both of them trussed up as they were. Hinderbrook had most of his body atop Tolburt's, and… Raedrick did a double-take. Hinderbrook's mouth and chin were covered in blood. And Tolburt had…teeth marks?…on the side of his neck.

"Get off him!" the senior guard - a Corporal like Raedrick - ordered, taking in the scene faster than Raedrick had.

The junior man bent over to pry the two of them apart.

"You promised me special treatment," Tolburt said, looking desperately up at the senior guard as his man grabbed at Hinderbrook. "Please."

The senior man snorted, then grinned viciously. "Don't worry, you'll get it." His grin widened. "Captain says you're to hang last."

The junior man finally managed to tear Hinderbrook off of Tolburt, whose face had gone ashen in the torchlight as his mouth dropped open in shocked horror, but the struggle caused him to overbalance and he fell back atop two others of Raedrick's men. They squirmed overtop him similar to how Hinderbrook had done with Tolburt. One of them slammed his forehead into the guard's nose, and he cried out in pain.

The Corporal cried out in chagrin and dashed forward, flailing at Raedrick's men with the torch. They backed off quickly, rolling away from the downed guard, but one of them - Shermyn Raedrick thought - had a wicked burn on his right cheek as a result.

The two guards backed away, the Corporal waving his torch threateningly. "To bed, you lot," he ordered hotly, though he sounded more disturbed than resolved to Raedrick's ear. He clearly had not expected any actual resistance from them.

Raedrick's men stopped moving, their eyes lowered submissively, and after a moment the Corporal harumphed and nudged the other man with his elbow. Then the two of them left, heading back down the picket line toward where they had their little campfire for the night.

For a time, the only sound was that of a man weeping.

Raedrick was sure it came from Tolburt. Then Raedrick heard Shermyn's voice, whispering. It made his heart leap.

"Corporal, I got his knife from his belt."

It took an eternity for Shermyn to cut Laremy free, and an even longer eternity for Laremy to cut the rest of the squad free as well. All except Tolburt and those closest to the guards. It would not do for those two to see Raedrick's men skulking about, not until it was too late to do anything about it.

A quick consultation later, Laremy and Kilfer crept up on the pair of guards. They were huddled around their campfire. The Corporal had his back to Raedrick's men, even.

Laremy took out the private with the knife, making quick work of him from behind. Kilfer was even quicker. The large man engulfed the Corporal in his meaty arms and snapped his neck with a quick twist of his shoulders. And then there was nothing standing between Raedrick's men and their freedom.

Elation spread through the group, and before Raedrick knew what was happening, a trio of them had gone to the campfire and retrieved brands. They set off through the camp, lighting tents ablaze while Laremy freed the last of the men.

"No!" Raedrick tried to shout for his men to stop. There was no need for this; they could just disappear into the night and no one's the wiser.

But it was no use. The day's terror and despair had given way to elation, and then raging bloodlust and a desire to make the people pay who had caused them to feel such fear. In moments, a half dozen tents were ablaze. Men screamed from within. Some tried to flee. A few made it unscathed, coughing and gagged from the smoke. Others emerged from their sleeping gear fully ablaze, their screams eclipsing the worst sounds Raedrick had ever heard, and he thought he had heard them all on the battlefield.

But there were many more tents in the Company that captured

them, and within moments the rest of the troops spilled out. They were dressed in their small clothes, most of them, but they brandished weapons, one and all.

It only took a moment for them to recognize the source of the attack, and they came running. First in ones or twos, and Raedrick's men managed to overcome them. But quickly, squad leaders and officers got their men coordinated, and they advanced as a unit.

"We've got to get out of here," Hinderbrook said, standing at Raedrick's side. He bore a longsword that he had taken from one of the solitary soldiers who had come against them, but he was bleeding from a gash on his shoulder.

Raedrick nodded. "Retreat!" he called, and the closest of his men complied.

Others, too close to the advancing soldiers, were not so lucky. One fell the moment he turned to run. Two more hefted newly-liberated swords and went back-to-back, their faces grimly determined. Raedrick knew that expression - there would be no surrender; they would go down fighting. In the end they were dead anyway, so why not?

Hinderbrook grabbed Raedrick's shoulder, spinning him away from the fight. He was right; there was nothing Raedrick could do except get killed himself. It was time to go. He began to run.

"Corporal!"

Tolburt's voice brought him up short. He turned and saw the youngster, still bound to the picket line. His eyes were wide with terror, and he looked at Raedrick desperately.

"Corporal, help me!"

Raedrick hesitated.

"Corporal!" Hinderbrook shouted, from next to him.

Raedrick barely heard him. Tolburt looked so scared.

"Raedrick!"

Something struck him across the face and he stumbled a step backwards. Hinderbrook recovered from the slap and grabbed Raedrick by the shoulder again.

"We need to go now." Hinderbrook glanced back at Tolburt and spat. "He's getting what he deserves."

Raedrick opened his mouth to protest. He could not leave his man behind. But Hinderbrook shoved him backwards, shouting, "Move!"

Raedrick took two stumbling steps away, then looked back. Tolburt lay squirming in his bonds, desperately. Their eyes met. "Corporal! Please!"

His two men who were fighting back-to-back had fallen. The rest of the soldiers were advancing toward them. Hinderbrook was right. It was time to go.

He turned and ran, Tolburt's last despairing plea seeming to chase him through the night as he went.

7

RISE AND SHINE

Raedrick awoke feeling fuzzy-headed; his sleep had not been particularly restful. Those memories intruding on his dreams prohibited it. For a few seconds, as he lay there in the darkness, he considered just forgetting the silly notion of heading up into the mountains after this man and going back to sleep. But duty called, so he pushed himself up to a sitting position and rubbed at his eyes, removing the last sleep from them.

At least he did not have a headache. His mouth was dry and a sour taste lingered on his tongue, but aside from the slightly-fuzzy feeling that comes from inadequate sleep, his head was fine. Better get moving before that changed.

He forced himself up, went through his morning routine - abbreviated a bit - and snarfed down some dried fruits as a quick breakfast. In just a few minutes he was out the door of his little flat, dressed in his thickest winter coat and leggings, several layers of thinner cloth beneath each, his gloves and cold weather hat, and overtop it all his pack and a thick wool cloak. It was a damn sight more appropriate for the elements than what he had been wearing the day before, but he had no illusions that he would be anything but cold on the side of the mountains.

He considered bringing his sword but quickly shelved the

notion. This was a rescue, not an assault. The sword would just get in the way and be extra weight to carry. So he left it behind, taking a long dagger in its place.

His flat lay less than a block from The Oarlock, on the same street as the Inn. He would pass it by as he set off for the Healers Circle. For a moment he considered stopping and going in. Molli and Lani were almost certainly up already, getting ready for the day, or closing out the previous one depending on how busy the place had been last night. It would be good to speak with them...with her.

He pulled his flat's door to and locked it, then turned and froze still.

A young woman, maybe twenty years old, stood outside his flat, her arms crossed over her chest, and not just from the cold. She was bundled up for the cold but even with those layers it was obvious she had an impressive figure. Only a bit shorter than Raedrick himself, she had flowing blonde hair and hazel eyes. Her heart-shaped face was marred by a frown that was, unless he missed his guess, brought on by worry...and a bit of irritation.

"You were going to go without saying goodbye?" Lani asked flatly.

He did not ask how she heard about the expedition. Lani heard everything, and oftentimes well before he did. "We won't be gone for more than a day, maybe two. It's hardly goodbye."

Her tone grew more heated. "I've lived here my whole life, Raedrick. I've seen more than my fair share of men leave on day trips in the middle of winter and never return." She drew herself up. "And you know it."

Raedrick's cheeks grew hot as he flushed slightly in embarrassment. Of course she would not buy into that argument. She knew the perils of the mountains far better than he did. He sighed. "I'm sorry. I didn't want to worry you."

She voiced a very unladylike curse in response to that. "So you thought my not knowing where you were would make me worry less?"

Raedrick had no response to that. In truth, he had not given Lani, or her mother for that matter, a whole lot of thought. His mind had been focused on his new mission, and on getting ready for it. Everything else…

But that was not entirely true. He knew Lani would worry, but he also knew - or rather suspected - that she would try to stop him. And he had not been sure he could hold out against her attempt.

Silence lingered for several seconds while he tried to get the words together to understand. Then Lani sighed.

"Why are you doing this, Raedrick?"

"There's an injured man up there who needs help."

She shook her head. "No. Why are *you* doing this? You could have hired Povol and his pals," she was good; did she know all the details of his plan? "to search the mountains and report back to you. That's what Malory always did, and it worked out fine." In the semi-darkness, she leaned forward, peering at him. "Why are you going out there personally? You don't know anything about how to get around and survive in the mountains."

That was not completely true. He had plenty of training, and more experience, on surviving in the wild, in all sorts of conditions. But the Saddleback Mountains in the depths of winter were not just any set of conditions; they were some of the harshest conditions a man could face anywhere in the Kingdom. And he intended to go right into their teeth.

Put that way, it did not make a whole lot of sense.

Raedrick took Lani's hand gently and gave it a little squeeze. "It's something I have to do." He told her about Tolburt, all of it, and her features softened. Somewhat. "I left him behind then, to save myself. If I help his friend, maybe…" He swallowed. "Maybe that will make amends. A little."

"You left him. After he betrayed you. I don't think you owe him anything."

The same argument Julian had made. They did not understand. "He was one of my men, Lani." He shrugged slightly,

47

looking away, toward where the Healers Circle lay. "A commander does not leave one of his men behind."

She was silent for a long several seconds, absorbing his words. He did not look back at her, for fear that her disapproval would have grown worse. He was not sure he could deal with that, on top of everything else.

Suddenly, she embraced him, squeezing him fiercely. He was so surprised he did not return the embrace for a few seconds, so sure was he that she was only growing more angry with him. Finally he held her, and it seemed they stood there like that for an hour, though in truth only a few seconds passed.

Nestled against his shoulder, she spoke softly. "Don't you go and do something stupid up there, Raedrick Baletier. I could not stand it if anything happened to you."

A sound that was half-snort and half-chuckle, from behind them, interrupted before Raedrick could reply. "Fat chance of that, Lani. I don't think I've ever seen him *not* do something stupid, once he decided to get all heroic in the head."

Julian stepped into view. Like Raedrick, he was dressed in overlapping layers of wool and fur, gloves and a cold weather hat, a pack, and stout boots. Unlike Raedrick, he bore a bow and quiver slung over his shoulder. He smirked playfully and gave Lani a little wink.

She gave a little start at seeing Julian and stepped away from Raedrick, pushing a lock of hair back away from her face. If Raedrick had to hazard a guess, he would say she was embarrassed.

"Hello, Julian," she said. "Are you going off on this mad hunt as well?"

He shrugged. "Looks that way." His eyes left her and traced down the street, toward where The Oarlock lay, a small circle of light in the otherwise mostly dark street. They kept the lamps outside lit all night, and depending on the night kept serving all night as well. "Getting started early this morning?"

She shook her head. "Just getting off. The Tanlyson brothers played last night, and the crowd demanded several encores." She grinned, but the grin was overcome by a yawn a moment later. "Figured I could catch this lump before he slinked away if I waited long enough."

Julian chuckled. "She's got you figured out, Rae."

"Seems like it."

They stood in silence for a couple handfuls of seconds. Then Lani inhaled softly and nodded briskly to each of them. "Well," she said, her voice steady, tightly controlled, "be careful up there." She opened her mouth, as though to say something more, but instead just shook her head and stepped around them. "Good luck," she said over her shoulder. Then she vanished into the slowly lessening gloom.

Raedrick watched her walk away, an ache in his heart that took him by surprise. He truly did not want to cause her concern, but he had a job to do. He sighed and turned back toward Julian.

His friend regarded him with a frank expression. "You're going to have to get that figured out pretty soon, Rae. She won't wait on you forever."

Raedrick flushed and coughed into his fist. This was not something he wanted to discuss right now. Or maybe at all. He cared for Lani, but... No, this was not the time. He squared his shoulders and cleared his throat, forcing his thoughts back to the business at hand.

"Thought you weren't coming."

Julian snorted. "Last time I let you do something on your own, you almost got yourself run through." He flashed a grin that Raedrick found himself returning in kind, angst over Lani's state of mind fading somewhat to the background.

He nodded and clapped Julian on the shoulder. "Let's get to it."

8

UP THE HILL

At least the weather was better.

The wind had died down to a gentle breeze with occasional brisk gusts and the overcast had broken up. The moon was clearly visible in the eastern sky, a shining crescent a thumb's breadth above the mountains that would be its home for the day, and dawn was beginning to break, pink and lovely, in the west, illuminating only a few high altitude clouds in the sky overhead.

"Going to be a nice day," Raedrick said.

"About time. I thought that blow would never end." Julian squinted up at the rapidly brightening sky and grinned. "Maybe this trip won't be so bad after all."

Raedrick hoped he was right.

They picked up Sebastini at the Healers Circle, then hurried over to Povol's place of business.

The mountaineer had a fair-sized house in the northwest corner of town, and an above average tract of land to go with it. Behind the house, which was just a single story but seemed to loom nevertheless, he had fenced off a large area and set up a number of small buildings: the houses for his dogs.

They were already up and about as the three men walked up to Povol's property. Barks and yips, and the occasional growl, reached Raedrick's ears easily, and he immediately understood why Povol's place was as separated from his neighbors as it was. He for sure would not want to be the one who lived next to that. Not unless he had to be up extra early every day.

They found Povol around back, near his dog pens. The mountaineer was bundled up even more than they were, though much of his bulk came from his pack and the numerous tools and strands of rope that hung from a thick leather harness fastened over his outer coat. He was busily fastening his dogs to leads that were attached to long, narrow sleds. Five dogs each, for three sleds.

Povol glanced up as they approached, and nodded. "You're late, Constable."

Raedrick raised an eyebrow. "Seeing as you are just now ready to go, I'd say we're right on time."

Povol snorted out a half-laugh and stood. He scratched behind the ears of the dog he just attached and looked the three of them over for a moment. Then he shook his head. "Didn't know he was coming along," he said, nodding at Sebastini.

The guildsman replied, "I have been up in the mountains many times, Povol."

"I know that. But I've only got three sleds." He considered Julian and Raedrick then, frowning. "Either of you ever drive a dogsled?"

Raedrick shook his head. He had seen some of the townsfolk - those few who actually left town during the winter - getting around on sleds similar to Povol's. He recalled thinking them ingenious, but he had never taken the opportunity to learn about them, or ride on one.

Julian, surprisingly, nodded. "Horace's friend Lommy took me out one time and showed me how to work his."

Povol smirked. "So basically no." He sighed and ran a hand along his pate, considering. Then he apparently came to a decision, as he nodded briskly and turned to Sebastini. "You'll ride with me then, Ravi. I don't want your extra weight to throw them off while they get the hang of it."

Sebastini nodded acceptance.

"Ravi?" Julian asked.

Sebastini chuckled. "You've never asked my given name, but I *do* have one."

Raedrick could not help but chuckling in return. He had never bothered to learn Sebastini's name either. The momentary sense of humor he felt faded as he asked himself the next question: Why not?

Povol interrupted that train of thought. "Ok, let's get your bags stowed and mount up. Daylight's wasting."

The sun was just beginning to edge up over the mountains to Glimmer Vale's west, but Povol had a point. The days were very short up here, and Stefan did not have much time.

They made better time than Raedrick would have thought. Sure, he had seen others driving their sleds around, and he could tell they made a good clip. But that was always from a distance. Actually being on the sled, he was immediately impressed by the device's effectiveness.

The group set out heading due west, along the path to the ford across the Northflow, or at least along where the path may have been come the Spring thaw. For now, they simply stayed away from the largest of the rolling hills that made up the terrain around Lydelton and pointed at the rising sun.

When they stopped at the Northflow, it was clear the river still flowed. Though water along the river's banks was frozen, the middle remained free of ice, and the current gurgled along nicely. Raedrick had never used this ford before, but if it was anything like the ford for the Eastflow, they had a good foot of near freezing water to wade through to reach the other side.

So much for using the dogsleds for very long.

But Povol surprised him. When Julian voiced the same concern Raedrick had, he shook his head. "It's only about five or six inches at this time of year." Then he dismounted and pulled open a satchel that lay on the front of his sled, in front of where Sebastini sat. From within, he pulled out a number of long, narrow oilskin contraptions which he proceeded to slip onto his dogs' feet and tie in place. Then he produced similar, larger, leggings for himself and Sebastini. The old man got up and donned the leggings without a word.

When they had prepared, Povol gestured toward Raedrick and Julian's sleds. "You have the same gear. Watch where I go and do exactly what I do."

Raedrick nodded, and immediately Povol gave a little command and his dogs set off at a slow walk. Povol walked beside the lead dog, holding his - Raedrick presumed the dog was male - collar and speaking softly, reassuringly Raedrick presumed, in his ear.

Sedastini walked at the rear of the sled and helped guide it into and out of the water while Povol guided the dogs across the ford. The oilskin garments worked well, and the water never got high enough to flood them out. So when they reached the far bank and removed the leggings, both men and dogs were dry, as though they had not just crossed a river.

Or at least as dry as they could be from stomping through the snow for the previous half hour.

"You won't need to lead them," Povol called, from the far side of the river. "They will come to me, so you should stay in the rear. Just make sure the sled does not get swamped."

"Seems easy enough," Julian said, from Raedrick's right. He had a profoundly skeptical look on his face.

"Yeah."

"You want to go first?"

Raedrick looked at his friend, so fearless in so many situations, and was surprised at his hesitation. He thought it over for a moment, then nodded.

The look of relief on Julian's face - relief that he did not have to be the pioneer on this one, unless Raedrck missed his guess - said all that needed saying.

In reality, Julian need not have worried. Raedrick made it across easily and quickly. Proving their masters' word true, the dogs went right to Povol when he whistled for them. The only things Raedrick had to do was keep the sled from getting stuck in the slushy mud at the bottom of the river and wave at Julian to hurry up.

Julian made the crossing with equal lack of incident. A few minutes later, after they got the oilskin garments packed again, the group got back to making time across the solid ground and its layer of snow.

After the ford, they turned north by northwest, veering away from the Northflow and entering the western reaches of the Glamorwood.

The trees closed in around them quickly, evergreens that stood high above them and collected snow in their branches but kept the canopy beneath more free of snow than the plains had been. Except where branches had given way beneath the weight or the wind had blown the snow off. There, the area below the trees was a mess of randomly piled snow and the occasional downed limb.

There was no trail that Raedrick could detect, but Povol led them without hesitation, choosing his turns as though he had been driving this route for his whole life. For all Raedrick knew, he just may have been. Few people from outside settled in Glimmer Vale. This past year had been novel, with Raedrick, Julian, and Melanie taking up residence. And not just because they were two fighting men - Constables now - and a renegade mage. It was entirely possible that Povol had never been farther abroad in the world than the borders of this Vale. But within... Well, there was no one who knew these mountains better, or so the word around town went.

So far, Raedrick had seen nothing to dissuade him from that opinion.

They passed an interminable amount of time beneath the canopy of the Glamorwood. Raedrick found himself shifting uncomfortably after a little while over memories of his last visit to these woods. Granted, the events involving that Out-Dweller and the mad Mage Telurian had taken place on the other side of the Northflow, but the woods here looked almost identical. He almost expected to see, jutting out of the earth atop a small hill ahead, the spur of rock where, three months ago, they had found the mutilated body that set them on their course against Telurian. It was foolishness, but all the same he could not shake the feeling that events were repeating themselves.

The terrain became more hilly, and their pace slowed as the dogs adjusted to the greater incline. But the animals were well-trained and they kept on pulling steadily. And then, all at once, as they rounded the curve of the up-slope of the steepest hill they had encountered yet, they burst out from beneath the trees and back into direct sunlight.

The transition was quick enough as to be stunning. The mountains, now looming all around them and covered in the winter's snow, were nigh-on blinding they reflected the sun so well, and Raedrick had to raise his hand to shield his eyes.

Ahead, Povol stopped his sled, but Raedrick almost missed it in the glare. He jerked his contraption to the right and almost overbalanced before he was able to come to a halt. Julian, meanwhile, stopped alongside Povol without difficulty. Both men looked at Raedrick with bemused expressions on their faces. Sebastini's quickly suppressed chuckle was even worse, but somehow not as bad as the amused twinkle in the old man's eye.

"Well," Povol said after a short pause. He gestured toward the mountain directly ahead. It loomed, taller than the others around it, like a great, curved tooth from some giant predator. "That's Tollard's Peak." He frowned up at the mountain, looking for a moment like a man sizing up an opponent. "That mountain will kill you quick, if you let it."

"Sounds like my kind of place," Julian said, wryly.

Povol turned the frown on him. "No. It isn't."

Julian's expression lost its amusement, and he nodded.

"But we're not actually going up Tollard's," Raedrick said, fishing the map Tolburt drew out of his pocket and unfolding it. "Stefan is holed up to the north, from the look of this."

Povol glanced at the map and smirked. "Like I told you last night, that thing isn't precise." He turned back to the mountain and pointed to the east. "There's a deep valley, more like a canyon, that runs along Tollard's northeastern flank. That's where the Northflow runs. Can't go through there without a whole lot of climbing tackle and even more time." He swept his hand across the mountain's face, pointing to its western side. "The western face is all boulders and bad trails. Take us a week to pick our way through there. So…" He turned back to Raedrick and raised both eyebrows. "To get where we're going, we pretty much have to go straight ahead."

"Over the bloody mountain?" Julian sounded completely incredulous. "Are you serious?"

Povol shrugged. "It's that or go home. We won't make for the summit, just the shoulder above the canyon. It's not *too* bad an approach."

Raedrick looked up at the mighty peak, and the narrow - or at least it looked narrow from this distance - band of unbroken snow that led upwards and to the right, passing sheer cliff faces and obvious rocky patches across the mountain's eastern shoulder, and shuddered. This was not exactly what he had in mind.

"There's no other way?" He did not completely succeed in removing all hint of dismay from his voice.

"Not unless you want to circle way that hell around and come from another direction."

Stefan did not have time for that. Hell, he might be dead already if he was as badly hurt as Tolburt made out.

Raedrick sighed, then nodded his acquiescence. "All right. Let's climb a mountain."

Povol just grinned at him.

9

CAMPING OUT

The sun was low on the eastern horizon, only a hand's breadth above the mountains, and they were about a third of the way down the northern side of the mountain's flank when they found the tracks: a single line of footsteps that ran from east-southeast to the northwest. The unexpected discovery brought them up short, and they disembarked their sleds to investigate.

Povol frowned, crouching down next to the trail and studying the tracks with a practiced eye. "These are fresh. Definitely made today."

Raedrick was no tracker, but he had to agree. Yesterday's high winds and snowfall would have quickly filled in any tracks left then. Today's winds were less, especially here in the lee of the mountain, despite the occasional fierce gusts.

"None of your friends came up here today, did they?"

Povol shook his head and stood. "Whoever made them, he came from that way," he nodded to the east. "Not much there until you hit the canyon in a mile or so." He straightened his cloak around his shoulders and turned back to his sled. "Could be someone found your man already. Could be someone else we don't know about."

Raedrick shared a look with Julian. If someone had found Stefan, and then left... He could tell that Julian was thinking the same thing he was.

"I'm sure he is fine," Sebastini said, his tone firm despite the fatigue in his face. The day's climb had been hard on the older man, but he bore up well, not complaining at all.

Julian cast an incredulous look at the guildsman, who shrugged and spread his hands helplessly.

"Hope is better," he said simply. Then he turned around and settled himself back onto Povol's sled.

The mountaineer helped Sebastini get situated, then looked at Raedrick, an eyebrow rising questioningly. "Well?"

Raedrick nodded toward the east. "Let's check it out."

———

They found the camp in about twenty minutes. It was arranged in gap between a collection of boulders and a cliff face that came up on them seemingly from out of nowhere. One moment they were guiding their sleds down a gentle grade that curved around the mountain's flank, and the next they rounded a bend and found themselves at the foot of the cliff, which stretched a hundred feet or more above their heads.

The tracks led along the cliff face for a hundred yards or so, then vanished.

"Looks like this is the place," Julian said as they got off their sleds and followed the last of the tracks between the rocks.

Someone had obviously laid up here for a while. The area was mostly clear of snow; either cleared out or packed down to a near solid firmness. Leftovers of what looked like a meal littered the area: a few small bones and scraps of fruit skin. In the corner nearest the cliff face lay the remnants of a campfire; just blackened coals now, but Raedrick imagined for a moment that he could feel the fire's warmth. The faint odor of woodsmoke still lingered the in air, but then he was probably imagining that as well.

"Good place," Povol said, nodding in approval. "The cliff keeps most of the winds off you, and the rocks block the rest. Put a roof up and you could live pretty well here."

Julian looked askance at him. "We're going to have to discuss what you mean by living well."

Povol smirked back. "Not freezin' to death, boy."

Julian frowned, then shrugged after a short moment, apparently taking Povol's point.

"This cannot be where your man Tolburt left his friend," Sebastini said, eyeing Raedrick in confusion. "If he succumbed to the elements, his body would be here. If not, he would be here alive." He frowned, then shook his head.

Raedrick was forced to agree. All the same... He pulled Tolburt's map out again and looked it over. "This is the right location, isn't it Povol?"

Povol shrugged. "Can't say from that," he said. "Told you before it's rough. Could be dozens of hidey-holes like this around here." He paused. "Probably are."

Raedrick snorted. "You know everyone who would likely have come up here recently."

Povol nodded.

Silence followed. Raedrick just stared firmly at Povol. He really did not have to be this obtuse; what was he playing at?

Finally, Povol nodded again, sighing in resignation. "Ok, point taken. No one else was up here. At least no one from town."

"Other people live in the Vale though, Rae," Julian said. "At least as many as in Lydelton itself."

"Yes, but they are mostly farmers or ranchers. How many of those sorts of people go gallivanting around the mountains in the middle of a snowstorm?"

He turned and left the little campsite, folding up the map and replacing it into his pocket.

Julian followed along behind him. "We going where I think we're going?"

Raedrick pointed at the footprints leading away northwest from the campsite, and nodded.

The tracks led a straight path, or as straight as a path could be on the side of a mountain. They led generally northwest and downward, toward a valley between Tollard's Peak and its neighbors, mountains that only looked diminutive when compared to the monstrosity that was Tollard's.

The snow was surprisingly shallow, and well-packed. The tracks they followed were only slightly depressed, and the sleds' runners did not penetrate even as deeply as they.

"It's frozen solid beneath," Povol said when Raedrick asked about it during a brief stop to re-tie the leads on one of Julian's dogs' harness. "It never gets very warm up here, even in summer." He raised an eyebrow, glancing up at the surrounding peaks as he worked on the line. "Ever notice how many of the mountains are snow-covered year-round?"

He had, though he never thought about it before. "Yes, now that you mention it."

Povol grinned wryly. "Some melts and runs off, but most stays. New snow falls in the winter," he pulled the lead tight and stood, clapping his hands together quickly, "and the stuff beneath freezes."

"So we're standing on a sheet of ice," Julian said, suddenly looking uncertain about the situation.

Povol nodded. "Let's get back on the trail."

An hour later, with most of the sun below the mountains to the east and the temperature starting to drop, Raedrick started looking around for places to hole up for the night. It did not look promising; they had descended probably a thousand feet, maybe more, and the grade had lessened considerably, but the flank of the mountain was still just a bare expanse of snow, broken only by the occasional rocky protuberances and cliff faces. He thought he could see some trees ahead, down in the valley, but that area was already covered in shadow and it was difficult to tell for certain.

They could not keep on like this through the night, though. They would blunder over a cliff, run into a boulder, or just fall over from exhaustion and the cold.

Cold. That was something he had almost become used to. And of course, he had not thought to bring materials for a fire. Neither had Julian, and he had not seen any fuel on Povol's sled either. So it was not like they had any prospect of not being cold, no matter what.

He urged his dogs to greater speed, and after a minute or so pulled even with Povol's sled.

"We're going to lose the light soon," Raedrick said.

Povol nodded agreement. "I know a place, about a half mile ahead, where we can stop for the night."

Raedrick squatted against the growing wind and looked ahead. The shadows were lengthening, but he could see much farther than a half mile and he did not see anything that looked like shelter. "Where? I don't see anything."

Povol glowered at him for a second before turning his attention back to his sled, and his dogs. He did not say anything, but his expression said it all: *You hired me to be your guide. Why did you do that, if you already know it all?*

Raedrick ground his teeth, but bit back the anger that welled up in response to the mountaineer's attitude. He had every right to be proud of his abilities, and after all he was correct. He knew the mountains better than anyone. Or if not that, at least he knew them one hell of a lot better than Raedrick and Julian did. Or Sebastini, for that matter, though the old man had not second guessed Povol, or really any of them, during the entire trip. He was apparently content to sit back until his skills were needed.

A man could learn a thing or two from an attitude like that.

Raedrick let Povol pull ahead again and contented himself to following the guide. He knew what he was doing.

And boy, did he.

Raedrick knew he was gaping, but he could not help it. Beside him, Julian did the same, his mouth hanging open like a whore's bodice. Not that Raedrick had seen that many whores' bodices. Or really *any* whores' bodices or...

Ok, get it together.

But it was hard to listen to that particular thought.

He had followed when Povol stopped his sled near an innocuous rock outcropping and gestured for the rest of them to come along. The mountaineer's accusing look just a few minutes earlier had put to rest any doubts he may have had, or at least it had put to rest the notion of speaking them. But when Povol disappeared behind a fold of rock, Raedrick had balked, unable to comprehend what had happened.

Until he followed and saw the narrow crack, just wide enough for a man to walk through without catching his shoulders on the sides of the crack, that ran back into the rock face. Even looking at it straight on, Raedrick was sure he would not have noticed the crack from as little as ten or fifteen feet away.

That was surprising enough. But it was nothing compared to what lay within.

He stood, stunned, looking at a cavern as large as a good-sized house. Stalactites hung down from the ceiling, stopping about a foot and a half above Raedrick's head, but the floor was relatively smooth, with only a few rocks strewn around. The floor itself curled and flowed in irregular humps toward the rear of the cavern, which did not end so much as constrict until it became a crack again, far too narrow to squeeze through. The entire place was well lit by a half-dozen wall sconces that held oil lamps, and a pair of wooden shelves stood on the wall to the right, holding jugs, mugs, and bedrolls. A fire pit, with logs already laid out ready for burning, lay in the exact center of the cavern, and Raedrick saw there was another narrow crack in the ceiling above the pit that ran up out of sight. Very dimly, he thought he could see the last glimmers of sunlight at the extreme end of the crack.

"Bugger me," Julian breathed.

Povol turned away from lighting the final lamp and grinned wolfishly. "This is not my first night on this mountain, boys."

Clearly, but...

"Nice place," Sebastini said, stepping past Raedrick and Julian and giving the cavern a nod of approval. "How long have you been using it?"

Povol shrugged. "Ten years, give or take." He moved over to the nearest shelf and picked up a particularly large jug. Unstoppering it, he took a quick whiff from its contents. He pursed his lips, considering for a moment, then with a slight shrug he looked at Raedrick and Julian. "Mead? It's home brewed a couple months ago, but it's still good."

Julian grinned from ear to ear. Raedrick joined him.

❧ 10 ❧

A GALLANT RESCUE

If someone had asked him, Raedrick would not have believed it possible that he could spend a comfortable night, and get a good night's sleep, up on that mountain.

But once they got the dogs inside and lit the fire, the cavern became positively warm and festive. Povol not only had mead but also food stocked up, and very shortly they had full bellies and warm bodies. It was not long before Raedrick became extremely drowsy. He had the presence of mind to think it would be wise to set a watch, but before he could say anything about it he succumbed to the fatigue of a restless night followed by a vigorous day.

When he came to, the other men were already up and moving, though only Sebastini was visible, stowing the cavern's remaining stores and generally squaring the place away.

No one noticed he was awake for a minute or so, and he considered just rolling back over and trying to feign it for a bit, so good did it feel to just lie there, even on the cold rock. But there was work to be done, and a man's life to save.

Although, if Stefan had indeed been out there for two full nights without help, it was not likely he still lived. Unless he was the one who left those tracks. But if that were the case, it meant he was not injured, or at least not injured as badly as Tolburt claimed. That only left a couple of possibilities, and Raedrick did not like them. Not one bit.

He almost hoped Stefan was dead for a second.

Enough of that. He pushed himself up to a sitting position and rolled his shoulder to work out a kink for a moment before standing.

"Good to see you up and about," Sebastini said from over by the shelves, where he was replacing the implements of their night's stay.

Raedrick grunted. "How are we looking?"

The old man shrugged. "We can only hope Stefan found shelter as well."

"You think it was he who left the tracks?"

Sebastini shrugged again. "Time will tell."

"Not if we keep lollygagging around here it won't," Povol said, re-entering the cave just then. He looked Raedrick up and down and grinned at him. "We leave as soon as you're ready, Constable." Glancing at Sebastini, he added in the same playfully mocking tone he had used in Holb's when they first met, "If that is alright with your nursemaid."

Sebastini chuckled and passed Raedrick a plate filled with dried meats and fruits. "I would not let them wake you," he said, a half-apologetic smile on his face.

It was hard to be angry at that.

By the time he wolfed down breakfast and joined the other men outside, the sun had climbed well above the western peaks. Raedrick felt a momentary pang of guilt when he saw the time, but the rational part of his mind quickly pointed out that sleep was a weapon, and he needed to be at his best when they found Stefan. He did not let it enter his mind that they might not find him that day.

They got underway as soon as he got to his sled.

It was a good thing the weather had continued to be good overnight; the tracks still created an easily-followed trail that continued down slope toward the valley ahead. So they made excellent time.

Raedrick began to worry more and more, though. It had now been two full days, and getting well into the third, that Stefan had been up here without aid. How much longer could he last, if he had at all? How long should they keep up the search before simply declaring him lost? And as the tracks led them deeper into the valley and trees began to spring up again, sparse at first but becoming an actual forest up ahead, a bigger question reared: whose tracks were they following?

They stopped for a brief lunch alongside a small stream, mostly frozen over except for a narrow strip in its center where the running water kept the ice from getting a firm hold, and Raedrick found he was not the only one troubled about this turn of events.

"An injured man, unable to get food or fuel for a fire, could not last very long up here," Povol said, "so how much longer do you want to search?"

Julian shrugged and took a bite of dried beef, looking at Raedrick in that way he did that said he was deferring the answer.

Raedrick frowned. He had been mulling that over for a while and he had no good answers either.

Sebastini spoke up. "A man can survive for quite a while, as long as he has water." The old man swept his arm around, gesturing at the snowfield all around them. "Which is plentiful, right now."

Povol snorted. "Bigger concern's the cold." He turned frank eyes toward Raedrick. "If he made it through last night, he'll be hypothermic. No chance he lasts a third night."

"He could have found another cave like yours," Julian said.

Povol shook his head. "He didn't use my cave or we would have seen him, or signs of him, and the next good cave that could be shelter is a couple miles west, and upslope again. With a busted leg…" He left the rest unsaid.

"The trail we're following wasn't left by a man with an injured leg," Sebastini pointed out.

Povol shrugged. "Not much else to go on. Could be whoever left this trail found him, or was carrying him, or…"

"Or there's something else going on here," Raedrick said, interrupting. He sighed and looked down toward the valley floor, now just a mile or so away and a couple hundred feet below them, and covered in evergreens. A big part of his mind shouted that they should return to town, that Stefan was dead. If he had ever been up here at all. They only had Tolburt's word on what happened, and he had lied to Raedrick before.

But not about something like this.

No, about something much worse.

It was a not a choice he relished making. If they gave up too soon, he condemned Stefan to die slowly, either of thirst and hunger or from exposure. But they only had so many supplies themselves.

And then there was that big question of the tracks. He could not shake the feeling that he was missing something here, something important.

"What you wanna do, Constable?" Povol asked again. "Don't much matter to me; I get paid regardless. But…" He spread his hands, letting the silence finish the sentence for him. There was no chance they would be able to find this Stefan, if they had not already. They might as well head back to town and save themselves the trouble.

Raedrick was just about to voice reluctant agreement with Povol's unspoken sentiment. But then he glanced down toward the valley again, and noticed something new: a trail of smoke rising out of the trees, about a third of the way across the valley floor.

It should not have been a surprise, seeing that. They were following a man's tracks, and men always build fires in the sorts of conditions that prevailed up here in the mountains, at least once they were finished moving around for the day.

If the person who left the tracks was down there, they could catch up with him. And maybe he would be able to assist them in their search somehow. Or maybe Stefan was down there as well.

There was only one way to find out.

The scent of woodsmoke lay lightly upon the forest, growing steadily stronger as Raedrick and his party drew near to the campsite. The trees here were tall and thick of trunk; it had been decades since men had felled a tree here, if ever they had. Though they were spaced well apart, the trees were plentiful enough that they obscured vision past a few dozen feet. The forest itself was quiet, the accumulated snowfall less, the flakes having collected on the bows above instead of making it to the ground. All the same, as in the Glamorwood there were areas of unexpectedly deep snow and fallen limbs, slowing the group's progress.

It may have been smarter, and less hassle, to leave the sleds - and the dogs - behind shortly after they entered the woods and came across the first obstruction, but Povol would not hear of it. He had spent too much time and effort - and money - raising and training his dogs. He was not about to leave them out where they could be taken by a predator, or run away, or...

Raedrick looked askance at the mountaineer as he voiced that objection. "The dogs each weigh almost as much as a man. I think they can take care of themselves, maybe better than we can."

Povol snorted. "Not sure what you use to qualify a dog as a man."

Raedrick just stared at him, then repeated the request, more firmly.

Povol shook his head again, emphatically, and the look in his eyes told Raedrick to give over, because he would get nowhere with this.

So they continued on with the sleds, despite Raedrick's growing unease in doing so.

But why should he be uneasy? It was not like they were trying to be stealthy in their approach. They were on a rescue mission, not scouting out some enemy stronghold or something.

It must be the anniversary that had him jumpy...

Just like that, it struck him. He and Julian had not performed their remembrance ritual yesterday. He had meant to, but with everything that had happened it slipped away. He had not even thought about it. Guilt swept through him, guilt over forgetting to honor his men's sacrifice, and guilt over the betrayal he had lead them into.

Not that it had not been the right thing to do. He never doubted that. But doing the right thing carried a dreadful cost, a cost that he would have been fine paying himself. But to ask it of his men... And he had not even asked.

This was not the time to dwell on such things. He needed to keep his mind on the present, not wallow in the price for his actions. He shoved the guilt down, stifling it beneath a weight of will, but he was not able to make it leave completely.

Nor could he banish his own apprehension over the camp they were approaching.

From up ahead, he heard the pop of fresh wood catching fire, and then they rounded the trunks of a particularly large and closely-placed pair of trees and caught sight of the camp.

A quartet of men sat around the fire, which burned merrily and energetically within a makeshift fire pit the men made by stacking rocks of varying sizes together in a ring. They had set up a pair of spits over the fire, which held several animal corpses that sizzled and spat grease periodically, adding the pleasant aroma of meat that was nearly done cooking to the now prominent odor of woodsmoke that dwarfed the fresh scent of new snowfall that had mostly dominated the forest until now.

Raedrick halted his sled next to Povol and traded glances with him. The mountaineer gave a little shrug.

Might as well go and say hello.

The group dismounted their sleds quickly and set off on foot for the last twenty feet or so until they reached the edge of the camp.

Or at least, they meant to.

"Hold it right there," came a gravelly voice, from off to Raedrick's right.

He froze, turning his head slowly in that direction, but not before he saw the men around the fire turn swiftly toward the group, weapons in their hands and from their expressions completely unsurprised.

The voice came from a lean man who stood a head taller than Raedrick and was dressed in ragged furs and wools. He, too, was armed. And so were the three other men with him.

The man half-grinned, half-smirked, and the soft clearing of a throat from the left announced the presence of still more men.

Raedrick's group was surrounded, or near enough to it.

Wonderful.

✺ II ✺

UNDER ARMS

T he men spread out in a loose half-circle between Raedrick's group and their camp site. They numbered a dozen in all. To a man, they wore a ragged mixture of furs and wools that bore heavy grime from an extended time in the wild without cleaning. They all wore their hair long and most had rough beards that had not been trimmed in some time.

And they all brandished weapons: swords, a few axes, and two bows with arrows nocked.

A big, burly man with a protruding gut, salt and pepper hair, and a long bushy beard that reached nearly to his chest stepped forward. His left eye was fused shut by a puckered scar that ran down his forehead, across his left cheek, and to his jaw. He scowled at Raedrick and his companions, and the scar and missing eye gave the scowl a particularly menacing look. Had he never heard of an eye patch?

"Well, well. What have we here, boys? A few lost souls, wandering in the wilds, hmm?"

A couple of the men snickered, but made no other comment.

The speaker, apparently the leader of the group, spoke again. "What brings you four out here?"

Raedrick shared a looked with Julian, whose expression was

flat and guarded, as though he anticipated trouble. He held his bow in his left hand and his right lingered near his quiver, which hung from his hip opposite his long dagger. He was ready to throw down, but they could not stand against this many men, not at this range.

Raedrick took a step toward the leader, but stopped quickly when he noticed the sudden tension in the other men, the way the bowmen drew halfway back on their bowstrings, the sudden creak of leather as men adjusted their stances to be ready to move. This would require great care if they were going to avoid a confrontation.

"We're looking for someone."

The leader cocked his head to the side and licked his lips as though tasting Raedrick's words. "Looking? Found someone you have, I would say, hmm?"

Right.

He cleared his throat. "I'm Raedrick Baletier, one of the Constables of Lydelton." The tension within the men went up as soon as he said the word Constables, and Raedrick realized he just made a mistake. But the die was cast, might as well keep on. "This is Julian Hinderbrook, Povol Gerberson, and Ravi Sebastini, guildsman of the Healers Circle." Hopefully Sebastini's status as a guildsman would go a ways toward easing their tension. Few and far between were the men who did not esteem the Healers Circle. Even the most hardened criminals had been known to leave guildsmen be, or even offer them assistance. You never knew when you might need the Circle's assistance, and though they were known to treat all comers, there was an unspoken implication when one dealt with them that causing them offense might tarnish one's chances with them in the future.

On cue, the leader's eye widened a hair at Sebastini's introduction. Raedrick glanced behind at the old man and was pleased to see he had let his cloak fall open, revealing his distinctive white and gold coat beneath.

"We received word of a badly injured man in the vicinity, and we've come to bring him back to town for care. We saw the smoke from your campfire and thought you may have seen him."

"That right." The leader sucked on his lower lip for a second or two, considering Raedrick with a disdainful look. "Ain't no one injured here." *Yet*, the man's tone implied heavily.

Raedrick nodded, managing a polite smile. "We'll leave you in peace then. Good day." He made to turn back to his companions, but halted when the leader spoke again.

"What happened to this poor fellow?" His tone said he felt no empathy for Stefan's predicament at all. "What's he look like?" He smiled quickly, a fake smile that never touched his single good eye. "In case we see 'Im."

Get the hell out of here. Now.

Raedrick knew he should follow the voice of his instinct, but fleeing at this point would only tip the leader's hand, forcing him to start violence if that was his real intent. And perhaps Raedrick could still get his companions out of this without having to resort to a fight that they could not win. Not with the odds as they were right then.

Readrick looked at the leader and put on a sympathetic frown. "Fell in a ditch during the storm two nights ago. Broke his leg. He friend almost died bringing us the word."

The leader nodded, pursing his lips again. Except this time, his eye twinkled with something that was almost merriment but not quite. Something more…sadistic. "That sounds familiar," he said, suddenly grinning as he looked at a man halfway around the semicircle to his right, Raedrick's left. "Don't it, Stefan?"

Raedrick's blood turned to ice water when he heard the name.

Oh no.

Stefan, a skinny man of average height and no beard, chuckled. "Guess I should have bled him, Geoff," he said. "Damn. I thought the storm would finish him off. That little bastard is a lot more tough than we figured."

Geoff nodded agreement then turned his eye back to Raedrick. His grin broadened, but it did not convey good humor, only the promise of sadistic actions to come. "I've got a problem here, Constable," he said. "See, I can't really let anyone go and let folks know what we're doing up here."

"And that is what, exactly?" Raedrick asked, keeping his voice calm despite the rapid beating of his heart.

Geoff did not answer. He made a small gesture with his left hand, and the two bowmen in his group drew their bowstrings back and released in a single fluid motion.

Then things began happening very quickly.

12

BURSTING FREE

Instinct, honed by dozens of engagements in as many battles, sent Raedrick diving to the right. His shoulder hit the snow, and he tucked into a roll and bounded back up to his feet a heartbeat later with his dagger in his hand. The arrow whistled past him as he rolled, close enough that he felt the slight breeze that marked its wake. That was close.

A cry of pain went up behind him, but he did not have time to see who was hit. Two men - one skinny and quick the other taller, with more muscles, though it was hard to tell for sure under their winter clothing - threw themselves at him. Both bore longswords, but only the skinny one attempted anything even approximating a proper cut.

Raedrick ducked beneath the cut with ease, but that just left him open to the bull rush from the larger man. The wind left his lungs as the fellow tackled him to the ground, his arms wrapped tightly around Raedrick's torso.

Unfortunately for Raedrick's attacker, he did not manage to secure Raedrick's arms when he took him down. The bandit squirmed spasmodically and let out a squeaky cry that was half surprise and have despairing understanding as Raedrick plunged his dagger into the little dimple beneath his ear. And then he lay still.

There was no time to relish that small victory. The other man was still there, and there were ten others after him.

Raedrick's lungs burned and he had difficulty inhaling, but he could not focus on that either, not if he wanted to live.

The quirky swordsman thrust his blade down at him, a stream of sunlight glinting off the sharpened tip for a second as it descended.

Raedrick rolled to his right, pressing upward with his arms and lifting the dead man's body as he did. He felt an impact, strong enough that it nearly forced the body back down onto him, and then the tip of the swordsman's blade emerged from the front of the dead man's chest.

Raedrick threw his whole weight into continuing the roll, forcing the body to the ground as he rolled onto his right shoulder.

The swordsman issued cry of chagrin as he lost grip on his blade and stumbled, falling to one knee on the other side of the dead man's body.

That was the opening Raedrick needed. He pressed down against the ground and forced himself to his feet, finally drawing in a lung full of air as he did so.

To his side, his attacker was regaining his feet as well. But he was unarmed.

Raedrick took only a moment to regain his equilibrium, then he sprang forward, kicking out with the toe of his boot. The attack caught the swordsman on the bottom of his jaw, snapping his head backward jarringly.

The man let out a grunt, there was a sharp cracking of bone, and then he fell limply to the ground, stunned at least.

All around, grunts, curses, and screams filled the area. And with them...growls and barks?

Off to the left, Julian loosed an arrow that took one of the attacking men in the thigh, but two others leapt past him and got within arm's reach before he could nock another arrow.

Further back, Povol was crouched next to his sled, fumbling at the ties that bound his dogs with his left hand. An arrow had penetrated his right hand. The dogs snapped and growled, but could do little else.

Three more men were closing on Povol. There was no way Raedrick could get to his aid in time to help.

But there was no need. Povol had worked those knots countless times, and injured hand or no, he knew how they worked. A second before the men reached him, he pulled the final knot and barked - almost literally barked - a single command.

The five dogs who pulled his sled leapt forward as one, and the three attacking men went down in a writhing mess of fur, fists, axes, teeth, growls, curses, and screams.

This was no time to stop moving. Raedrick dropped to his knee and grabbed up the sword that had been dropped by the man who tackled him, scanning his eyes to the right.

Sebastini stood a few paces in front of Julian's and Povol's positions between two of the attackers, who held him by the upper arms in firm grips. Though his eyes were tight, with fear no doubt, the guildsman held himself erect and wore a perfectly calm expression.

One of the bowmen was down, an arrow through his throat. The other stood next to Geoff, who surveyed the goings on with a displeased scowl on his face that only grew worse when his eye met Raedrick's.

For a second they locked gazes, and Raedrick felt he could see into the man's soul, so bright was the burning heat in his eyes.

A soul that could very well have been his own, if circumstances had been just a little bit different, and certainly reflected what some of Raedrick's own men had turned into after they parted ways. Geoff was a man past the edge of desperation, a man willing to do anything, prey on anyone, to keep himself alive and fed for another day.

Geoff broke their stare first, letting out a roar of rage. He swung his axe, a long-handled double-bladed battle axe that made Raedrick want to wince inwardly, it probably weighed so much, and pointed it at him. "Shoot him!"

The bowman pivoted so he faced Raedrick, then drew back and loosed.

But Raedrick was already moving. He shoved himself to his feet and broke left, spinning a complete circle that sent his cloak whirling around him even as he retreated. He felt the cloak tug as the arrow passed through it, but it did not strike him.

He raced past the engagement between Povol's dogs and the three men, darting left and right, crouching and jumping to make himself a hard target.

Another arrow whizzed by, just in front of him, and he again dove into a roll.

Ahead of him, Povol pulled a long piece of wood from the front of his sled. It took a moment for Raedrick to realize it was a spear. But the mountaineer would not be able to wield it properly, not with his strong hand run through as it was.

"Run, Povol," Raedrick called, waving at him to move.

Povol turned disbelieving eyes at Raedrick and snarled. "Not a chance - "

One of the dogs let out a yelp of agony. A second followed suit, then a third.

Raedrick spun around to see two of the men shove the dead dogs aside and push themselves to their feet. Their buddy was beset by the last two dogs, but he still thrashed and kicked strongly.

Beyond them, Julian lay on his back, one of the attackers' swords at his throat. He had his hands raised, open and free of weapons, in a gesture of surrender.

The other of the pair who attacked Julian was hurrying forward, toward Povol and Raedrick, and the remaining bowman was drawing another arrow back and sighting in on Povol and Raedrick.

"Run!" Raedrick shouted again, and shoved Povol in the shoulder. Hard.

This time the mountaineer offered no protest. He ducked, turned, and ran, a heartbeat before the bowman's arrow sped through the air where his head used to be.

Raedrick glanced back at Julian and Sebastini, torn. He could not just leave them to these men.

But the final two dogs were dead, the third man from that group finding his feet, his face a bloody mess from where one of the dogs and been gnawing on him and eyes burning with murderous intent.

The other three men would be on Raedrick in a heartbeat, and the longsword he bore was both heavier than his Tyrashi blade and required different techniques than he was used to. He might have been able to take them together using *his* weapon - if the bowman did not end him first - but with the longsword?

Hating the decision, but knowing there was no other option open to him, Raedrick turned and ran after Povol, ducking left and right to put as many trees between himself and the men, whoever they were, as he could.

13

TAKING STOCK

The sword against his throat increased its pressure ever so slightly and Julian cringed back. Or he would have, had there been anyplace further back he could have cringed. He could not move his throat further from the sword than it was, not without doing something incredibly stupid and easy to anticipate. As it was he lay prone, his hands raised in surrender and his eyes fixed on those of the man holding the sword.

Those eyes burned with hate and bloodlust. That did not make Julian feel good about the odds of him surviving the next few minutes.

Around him, the rugged men - he was beginning to think of them as brigands in his own mind; maybe they were the leftovers from Isenholf's band - were taking stock, licking their wounds. And those wounds were extensive: three dead and three more badly wounded, from what he could tell by listening. Not too bad for a group one third of the brigands' size, and taken by surprise, no less.

The swordsman looked away from Raedrick, back toward the campfire, where Geoff had been standing, and called out, "What ya want me to do wit' 'im?"

"Do not harm him." That was Sebastini's voice. Knowing that

he lived made some of the tension in Julian's chest drain away. Some of it.

"You're in no position to dictate, Healer," said Geoff. Julian did not think he would ever forget that guy's voice.

Sebastini snorted. "Nor are you. You wish my services to see to your men. I wish for you to not harm him." He paused, meaningfully. "Like for like, Geoff. It is a fair exchange."

"Piss on that," said a different brigand whose voice Julian had not heard before. "Your guild treats everyone who comes to them."

"Indeed we do," Sebastini said. "But you did not come to us, or *request* for us to come to you. You assaulted my companions and I while we were attempting to see to the well-being of another. And now you threaten him, and myself as well." Julian could easily picture the satisfied smile that Ravi had to be wearing; it showed through in his tone as he spoke. "We give our services *freely*, Geoff. I am under no compulsion to provide you with any assistance at all."

Silence reigned for a long time, though faintly - very faintly - Julian thought he could hear Geoff and the other man talking quickly to each other.

Finally, after what seemed forever, a trio of footsteps hurrying through the snow announced the arrival of three more brigands. They came to a halt nearby but outside of Julian's view and paused for a few seconds, panting, before one of them spoke.

"They gave us the slip, Geoff."

"What do you mean they gave you the slip?" Geoff asked, his voice rising abruptly and his tone dangerous. "There's half a foot of snow out there! They can't hide their tracks."

The speaker cleared his throat and spoke again, sounding apologetic. "They circled around and crossed their own trail three times, then they veered off over yonder until they found bare rock." A brief pause followed and Julian imagined the man was shrugging helplessly. "We lost the trail."

"Bugger me," Geoff said.

"Last thing we need is them interfering," another voice - Julian thought it was Stefan - said. "If they can -"

"You think I don't know that?" Geoff interrupted. He sighed, then added, "Crap."

The brigand Geoff had spoken with earlier interjected, "That's another reason to keep him alive. Information. About his friends and about the town."

The sound of general concurrence followed, and Julian could almost see Geoff sighing and nodding.

"Let him up," Geoff ordered, and a very brief period of hesitation followed for a second or three. Then the sword left Raedrick's throat and a powerful man with a trio of star tattoos on his forehead pulled Julian roughly to his feet.

Even if he would have been so inclined as to leave Ravi to these men's hospitality, Julian could not have gotten far. A quartet of men stood in his immediate vicinity, watching his every movement. Good thing he had no intention of running, not without bringing Ravi along with him.

Geoff faced Julian from about ten feet distant. His scowl contained the promise of all many of torments that would not end any time soon. But instead, he said, "Looks like it's your lucky day." The scowl became a positively malicious grin.

A couple of the brigands chuckled. One of them tested the edge of a dagger against his thumb.

Julian swallowed, hard. This was going to be bad.

"I think we've lost them," Povol declared, then he flopped onto the rock next to Raedrick.

"Let's hope so. How's the hand?"

Povol raised the roughly-bandaged hand and shrugged. The dressing looking positively awful. Dirty, held in place only with a quick knot, Povol had already bled through it, so the thing was basically one big bloodstain. "Willam'll fix me up good as new," Povol said.

If we get to Willam in time, Raedrick did not say.

"We need to figure a way to get close to their camp again," Raedrick said instead.

Povol shook his head emphatically. "That's nuts. What do you hope to gain from doing something like that?"

Did he really not know, or was that just stress and shock talking? Raedrick drew a breath to keep himself calm, then he spoke. "We're going to get Julian and Sebastini away from those men, Povol."

A loud snort was Povol's first response. "They're both dead by now."

It was Raedrick's turn for an emphatic head shake. "They won't harm Sebastini. Men like that need the Healers Circle's assistance far more often than most, so they will not want to offend him. And as for Julian," he sighed, "we will just have to trust in hope."

Povol looked at Raedrick like he had never seen him before. "You're mad." Povol pushed himself up to his feet then stood there for a second, leaning on his spear and looking out and down toward the forest's canopy a few dozen feet beneath the ledge they occupied. Finally, he pointed to the east, where the sun was about to begin setting. "We need to get out of here while we still can. The sun will cover us if we go now."

Raedrick sent a firm stare Povol's way. "You came up here to rescue a man, Povol."

"And it turns out he didn't need rescuing. Your friend Tolburt fed you a line of crap and you fell for it like an idiot." He shook his head again, then turned and spat in the general direction of the enemy camp.

That stung, but the words were true. He had not questioned Tolburt's story, not even once. And he should have; he remembered how Tolburt was, even before all hope was lost.

Raedrick drew a deep breath. "That may be true, but that does not change our obligation to Julian and Sebastini." He stood as well, brushing off his hands onto his pant legs. "Put it this way. You leave now without even trying to find out their status and I'll tell the Mayor you did not fulfill your part of the contract." He raised an eyebrow. "No rescue, no money."

Povol spluttered in consternation for a few seconds. "But..." He jabbed a finger - at least he could work the fingers on his injured hand; that was something - at Raedrick's face. "That was never a condition of our agreement, nor was going on a suicide mission against a group of bandits. Damn it, I'm not a warrior."

Raedrick snorted. Povol could more than handle himself. In his brief tenure as Constable, Raedrick had heard of Povol's involvement in no less than five or six bar brawls, and he had never come out on the losing end. Of course, a bar brawl is a far cry from a fight to the death with a group of trained killers. That was something Povol had not prepared for, not the way Julian and Raedrick had. It was probably not fair to ask this of him.

But there was no one else. In his gut, Raedrick sensed that, whatever reassurances he had spoken to Povol, as soon as Sebastini stopped being of use to those men, they would leave him in a shallow grave. Same with Julian, if they had not killed him already.

He did not have time to dilly dally.

He squared his shoulders and put on his most commanding expression, looking Povol in the eye. "I am altering the deal, Povol. I only pray I don't have to alter it any further."

Povol traded glares with him for a long time. The mountaineer's nostrils flared with each breath as he clearly fought back a number of powerful emotions, but that was the only indicator aside from his scowl - and truth be told it seemed he preferred scowls to anything else so that was not much of a change.

Finally, he nodded and looked away, longingly, toward the setting sun and the safety that lay in that direction. "Alright, Constable, I'm in. But not for a suicide run, here?"

Raedrick returned the nod. "If we can't retrieve them without a good chance of success, you don't have to go on."

Povol looked sidelong at him, his lips pursing as he considered Raedrick's words. "You mean *we* won't go on with it."

Raedrick looked away from him, toward the slowly rising smoke from the brigands' campfire, now barely visible in the swiftly approaching twilight, but did not reply.

No matter what, he would not leave his men in captivity again.

14

INTO THE BREECH

It was well past twilight and on to full dark by the time Raedrick and Povol crept their way down from their rocky perch and to the brigands' camp site.

Or what had been the brigands' camp site.

The fire still smoldered, the glowing coals and last remaining flames clearly visible in the blackness between the trees, but it had clearly not been tended in some time. The snow around the site was trampled almost to a solid block, making it exceedingly difficult to determine what happened where and when.

The bodies were easy to find, though. Three men, lined up in a row with their hands crossed over their chests, all dressed in the haphazard attire that marked them as part of the brigand party. Raedrick breathed a sigh of relief to see neither Julian nor Sebastini among them, just the two men who had attacked Raedrick - his kick must have broken the second man's neck - and the fellow Julian shot through the throat. Of course, that left the question of what had happened to Raedrick's friends, but at least they were still alive.

Probably.

From off to the right, Povol let out a strangled curse.

Raedrick hurried over and immediately saw what had the

Mountaineer so chagrined. Povol's sleds still lay off to the side, where they had left the conveyances earlier. They were mostly intact, only the straps that clipped the dog teams to them having been cut. But that was not what had evoked the curse.

All of the Povols dogs were dead. Not just the five he had managed to free to join in the fight, but all of them. Their bodies lay stacked like cordwood on the other side of the sleds, tossed aside like so much refuse. And they were completely lacking in fur; the brigands had skinned them.

It was a perfectly sensible thing to do, with winter's heart fast approaching and every scrap of insulation possibly the difference between life and death by hypothermia. But understand it as Raedrick did, these were not wild animals or predators who were harassing a herd. They were trained dogs, a man's friend and companion.

And looking into Povol's eyes right then, seeing how they reflected the dimming red glow of the dying campfire, Raedrick knew those dogs were as dear to him as family.

"Those bastards," Povol growled through clenched teeth. He flexed his good hand on the haft of his spear and Raedrick imagined he could hear the wood groan ever so quietly beneath the strain of the mountaineer's grip.

"I'm sorry, Povol," Raedrick said, feeling the words a bit lame.

Povol's breathing faltered for a second, then he sniffed and lowered his head. A soft sound escaped his lips, and Raedrick realized with a shock that he was weeping, weeping for his dogs, his friends.

He backed away a few steps, then turned back to the campfire, leaving the mountaineer to his grief. He would only have resented Raedrick for witnessing it.

By the time Povol recovered himself and returned to Raedrick's side, he had found the trail the brigands - and their captives he hoped - took away from the campfire. It would have been exceedingly difficult to conceal the footsteps of eleven people in the snow; Raedrick could not even conceive of a way to do it, now that he thought about it. So the trail was plain to see even in the faint light of the dying campfire and the rising moon.

"That's way too obvious," Povol said. From the tone of his voice - dry and slightly sardonic - one would never have known he had just suffered a personal tragedy, but Raedrick did not deceive himself. Beneath the surface, the mountaineer seethed.

Almost as much as Raedrick did himself.

Not again. Not ever.

Raedrick nodded. "If I were Geoff, I would leave men along my back trail to ambush us if we followed."

"Unless you thought we went back to town."

Raedrick turned and looked at him seriously. "He is not that stupid."

In the faint light, he could barely tell when Povol turned to meet his gaze. But he did, and held it for several seconds before he nodded acknowledgement. "So what do we do?"

Raedrick chuckled mirthlessly, testing his dagger in its sheath. Memories of a dozen midnight excursions behind enemy lines sprang to mind as he turned away from Povol and began following the beaten path through the snow.

"We set off the trap."

Julian cracked his eyes open and instantly wished he had not.

The light, so intense it seemed to burn into his brain, made him duck away, or at least try to. It felt like a torch literally jabbed into his head while it was still burning. But that did not compare with the fire that blossomed all over his skin, growing all the greater the more fully awake, and aware of himself, he became.

A guttural groan, nearly a scream, escaped his lips before he could force himself to silence.

Memory flooded back, knowledge racing ahead of pain to reclaim his mind before madness had a chance to take hold, and he grimaced, forcing the cries down as he took control once again. He would not give the bastards the satisfaction.

He tried not to remember that he had been unable to keep that resolve for very long last night. Better not to focus on that. Focus on the now, and the future. Resistance and survival depended on not giving in to despair, on remembering himself and his mission.

The Army taught him that in the final stages of his training before he reported to Raedrick's squad, oh so long ago. The odds of being captured by the enemy were slim, but if it happened every soldier needed to know what was expected of him, how he should behave, and how to resist betraying his fellows even under the worst torture.

He had scoffed at the training, back then. No one would be able to get to him.

But he had never been put to the test, not like that. Not until last night. Now, feeling the aftermath - and remembering how eager he had been to sell his friends out, how easily the knowledge he had came to his tongue, how hard it was to avoid saying anything - he shuddered to consider having to endure that treatment again.

He did not want to betray Rae, or his new home. But it hurt so bad.

So bad.

He did not know how long he could hold out in the face of what Geoff's men had done to him, and that had only been an abbreviated session.

Something touched his forehead and Julian swiped at it, instinctively, knocking it away. It was only after he had done it that he realized his hands were not bound. In amazement at that discrepancy, he looked around wildly, only stopping when a blurry ball of color appeared in his confused vision.

"Julian."

The word, his name, was barely understandable.

He blinked, and his vision cleared somewhat. The voice - it was a man's voice - spoke his name again, and then the colorful ball sprang into focus.

It was Ravi's head.

The guildsman looked down at him with concerned eyes. But when Julian met his gaze after a few seconds, some of the concern left his face, and a half smile appeared.

"It's good to see you awake."

Julian blinked again, and would have sat up, but something

held him back. And then a new fire cut across his chest, making him clench his teeth to avoid groaning even as he sagged back against his bed. Or the ground. Or whatever it was he lay upon.

"Easy, my friend," Ravi said, laying a calming hand on Julian's chest. The fire seemed to fade at his touch. "Do not move too quickly."

Julian inhaled, then spent the next half minute coughing. He coughed so hard, for a second he thought he would be unable to draw another breath no matter how acute the need to breathe became. And then, all at once, the coughing stopped.

He gasped in air, grateful for ever scrap he could take in. Then he lay there, doing nothing but breathing, and let his muscles relax. After last night's agony and the fiery discomfort of the morning - was it morning? - It felt good just to do that.

"Where," another lesser cough stopped him in mid thought. "Where are we?"

Ravi shrugged and produced a wet cloth. As he used it to wipe Julian's brow, Julian realized that was what he had swiped away a moment ago. If Ravi noticed the look of guilt Julian tried to suppress, he did not mention it. "Our hosts' camp. Probably five or six miles northeast of where we met them."

Julian wanted to melt beneath the comforting warmth and wetness of Ravi's rag, but this was no time to lose his bearing. "That far..." He frowned, shaking his head. He had no recollection of walking that far. Or really, of walking at all. He only remembered the...treatment. And then a red haze, followed by the all-too-brief slumber that Ravi interrupted. "How did we get here?"

Ravi chuckled. "I walked. You," he winced. "You, they dragged behind on a pathetic excuse for a litter."

"Ah."

"We do not have much time," Ravi said, sudden intensity in his voice and his gaze lending extra weight to his words. "When they..."

Geoff's strong, gruff voice broke in, overpowering Ravi's soft speech easily. "How is our guest, guildsman?"

Ravi withdrew from Julian's side, turning a stern gaze on the man who had stepped into the tent - Julian only now realized that he was in fact lying within a tent, and a rather poorly maintained one at that. "Better than I would have expected, considering your definition of hospitality." His words were laced with deepest contempt, conveying a bitter rebuke.

But if Geoff noticed, or cared, it did not show from the impassive expression he maintained as he looked past Ravi toward Julian. "Good. It would be a shame to waste him."

Ravi scowled, but said nothing more. Julian noticed that he flexed his fingers in both hands, making fists and the releasing them quickly. So, he did not find it any easier to write off dishonorable or downright evil behavior than any of the rest of the civilized population did. That could be useful, for planning an escape.

Julian looked up at Geoff and tried to put every bit of contempt he could muster into his gaze. The outlaw just looked down at him, his face implacable, and if the reproach Julian was trying to send affected him in any way, it did not show.

Several long seconds went by, and then Geoff cracked a little smile, one that Julian supposed was meant to be ingratiating, or at least not menacing, but only came across as fake. "You've got spirit, I'll give you that," Geoff said. "Better to show some sense. How long can you hold out, hmm?" He leaned forward, seeming to loom over Julian's prone form. "What I'm asking isn't much."

Julian just scowled at him, trying hard not to show how tempting the notion of just giving in was.

Geoff studied him for another long moment then shrugged and turned back to Ravi. "Make sure he doesn't get too comfortable," he said. Then he turned and swept out of the tent. "We move in one hour," he called over his shoulder. And then the tent flaps fell into place behind him.

Ravi breathed a muted curse that took Julian by surprise. He did not know guildsmen ever heard that particular phrase, much less understood what it meant to use it properly. The old man, scowling, turned away from the tent entrance and back to Julian. He must have seen the surprise on Julian's face because he flushed and shrugged slightly. "Wasn't always a Healer," was all he said.

Over the next several minutes, Ravi gave Julian a long, gentle massage, interspersed with more washing with the blessedly warm water on the rag. That was all, but by the end of it, Julian felt amazingly better. He stretched, as much as he could with the bands holding his chest and thighs down - he finally figured out what they were in the middle of Ravi's treatment - and sighed expansively.

"I could swear you were a mage," he said, gratefully.

Ravi sniffed, actually looking affronted. "Please. I am a medical professional, not some overgrown adolescent who enjoys playing with shiny objects."

Julian blinked in surprise, but found himself without adequate words to respond to that description.

Ravi went on, "They did not actually cause any serious damage. One of those fellows knows his way around an apothecary. The solutions they used would have felt like they were burning your skin away," Julian shuddered at the memory, "but in reality they are not much more than a topical irritant. Easily washed away, with the proper ingredients."

"Thanks."

Ravi nodded, but frowned as he looked back at the tent entrance. "I fear it will be for nought in a few hours. Just an excuse for them to get started again."

"Let me worry about that."

Ravi looked askance at him. More than askance. The look he gave Julian screamed that the guildsman thought he must be insane.

Julian put on his best, most dashing smile and tried to adopt the most confident tone he could. "You need to find a way to get us out of here. Take note of their watch rotations, who does what in camp, how their sentries are laid out... The next time they let their guard down, or let up at all, we need to be ready to move. Quickly."

Ravi snorted. "There is an excellent chance you will be unable to go anywhere." His earnest face looked pained, and wary, as he leaned in closer to speak more quietly. "Why don't you just tell them? We really don't know much at all about them, and what they're up to."

Julian shook his head. "They're on the run. They'll never believe we don't know about them, or have a notion of what they're looking for, else why would we be up here? They have to think Tolburt told us everything about them already, and Geoff's all but certain troops will be right behind us. I'll never be able to convince him otherwise." He let out a sigh. "Besides, soon as he's decided I've told him anything, he'll kill me."

Ravi blinked at that, shaking his head in denial. "No. No, he promised your health in exchange for my services."

"Did he? *Really*?"

"Well...I thought..."

"Did he actually come out and say he would spare me, or was it just implied?"

Ravi frowned deeply.

Julian thought as much. He sighed again. "When the time comes, he won't hesitate. By then, you will have already treated his men. You've been seeing to them as well as me, yes?"

Ravi nodded, looking a bit sick.

"Well. There you have it." Julian pushed himself upward as much as he could within his restraints and fixed Ravi with his most stern gaze. "Of course, sooner or later, probably sooner, if he doesn't get what he wants, he'll decide to finish me, regardless. And maybe you as well, since you won't help him once I'm gone, will you?"

Ravi shook his head. He looked even more pale.

"In that case, we have to get out of here. And the sooner the better."

Ravi swallowed. Hard. He looked decidedly uncomfortable with the entire notion, but finally, after more than a few long seconds of consideration, he nodded acquiescence.

Julian managed a grin that he hoped looked confident. Time to get to work breaking out of here.

16

FORCED MARCH

Geoff was not kidding. Exactly one hour after he left, they were on the road again. Or they would have been, had there been a road. They trudged along in a rough line behind Geoff and another man - Stefan, Julian thought though he never got a good look at him to be sure. Three more of Geoff's men walked ahead of Julian and Ravi, blocking most of Julian's view ahead. The remaining four walked behind them, one of them with a pronounced limp from the arrow Julian had put into his leg.

Smart. Keep him and Ravi as closely surveilled, and as close to surrounded, as possible, to reduce chance of their escaping.

But then, where were they going to escape to, in the middle of the day, in the middle of the mountains? The fact that this particular problem factored largely into the plan he was trying to decide on was not lost on Julian.

The pace was brutal, all the more so because the bandits left the straps on around Julian's chest and shackled his arms behind his back using some contraption that attached his wrists to the straps. So he could not move his body naturally with his stride. He also could not pick his way past obstacles very well - Ravi ended up all but dragging him along in several places.

All that would not have been so bad if not for the fact that they were moving almost continually up hill. Very quickly, Julian was overheated despite the bitter cold of the mountain morning, and his breath came in rapid, ragged gasps. It was as though he could not get enough air down no matter how hard he tried.

The bandits did not talk much to each other, and never to the two prisoners, except to bark an occasional order or to grumble about the extra cost and reduced speed they incurred for keeping them with the group, or even alive at all.

It made Julian thankful that Geoff was in charge. He may have been a criminal, and an unrepentant one at that, but he was not uncivilized. At least not completely. Yet.

But how much longer could that last?

As they walked, Julian worked hard to keep note of where they were going, but also of what the bandits were doing, what they were saying, their demeanor and defensive posture, or really anything that could give him some advantage in planning or executing the escape. Or - and he hardly dared to dream on this one - if Raedrick and Povol were planning a rescue.

They emerged from the forest shortly after they set out and began ascending the smaller mountain to the north of Tollard's Peak. Julian had no idea the peak's name, if it even had one, and small as it was compared with Tollard's sheer boldness in stretching up to the top of the sky, it was easy to not realize that the peak was fairly lofty itself, with many cracks and crevices that could hide almost anything.

They stopped briefly near one of those cracks and crevices, a place where there must have been a rockslide at some point in the past. A number of boulders and smaller rocks protruded from beneath the snow, and the crack in the mountain face - Julian thought he recalled Povol talking about going up a chimney once and described it, but Julian had not really envisioned it well until now - was similarly filled. Julian supposed this spot would make a decent place for lunch, with good protection from the variable winds in the mountains.

But they did not have lunch. Instead, the bandits held a palaver. They crowded around Geoff and Stefan, speaking in low tones and referring to some paper that Stefan held in front of himself.

For a minute or two, it did not appear they would get anything decided until, finally, Geoff himself spoke out, loudly.

"Enough!"

The other bandits stopped talking. Geoff issued a series of terse orders, in a tone too low for Julian to fully make out more than a word or two. But what he heard was enough to figure out that Geoff was worried someone might be following them.

When the group set off again, two of their number remained behind, taking station in the crevices between some of the larger boulders. They would lie in wait and ambush anyone coming up behind.

This was potentially bad. Julian had no doubt Raedrick was following; he presumed Povol was as well. Normally, he would put Raedrick up against any two men and expect him to come out on top with barely a scratch. But he had not brought his sword with him. Julian had no idea how much experience Povol had, but he looked to be good in a fight.

That did not necessarily translate into his being good at killing, or at surviving an ambush.

He glanced over his shoulder once before they turned a corner that would bring them out of sight of the two bandits, trying to figure out a way to foil the ambush plan. But there was nothing he could do. A rough shove in the back from one of the bandits behind him confirmed that; it almost sent him sprawling, without his arms available to help him keep his balance. So he clumped along, going as slowly as the bandits would let him and hoping against hope that Raedrick and Povol would not be caught unawares.

By the time the sun reached the top of the mountains to the east, Raedrick and Povol's chances in the face of the brigands' ambush were the farthest thing from Julian's mind.

He only *thought* the previous night's torture left him exhausted and in pain. This day put the lie to that. When he was finally able to collapse onto his backside in the little bowl of rock the bandits - well, Geoff - chose for the night's camp site, he literally could not feel his legs, or his hands. The shackles that held his arms in place had dug into his wrists all day, and the awkward angle of his arms induced cramps in his shoulders and back. His cloak had flapped open early on, and by the end of the day, even with the layers he wore he could not shake the chill that seeped throughout his body. His legs... He never would have thought how much more difficult losing the use of his hands would make it to keep his balance. Especially as the grade they climbed became more steep, it was all he could do to put one foot in front of the other, and not fall over each time.

Ravi tried to help. He lingered back with Julian, giving him a hand as he could, but the guildsman was hardly muscle-bound, and the bandits would only let him help so much.

All told, it was pure misery.

On the bright side, Julian's inability to move steadily meant their pace slowed considerably throughout the rest of the after-noon. But that was small comfort. He was acutely aware of the annoyed looks the bandits cast his way. He could imagine the conversations going on with Geoff, up at the front of the column.

"Why are we keeping this guy with us?"

"He's just slowing us down."

"Best to bleed him and have done with it."

"Toss him off a cliff."

That last imagined suggestion made Julian's stomach lurch. The notion of falling and falling, for what he was sure would seem an eternity, of watching the ground come up to meet him, and knowing all the while that there was nothing he could do and his end was coming with that ground... He shuddered to think of it.

But there was a very real chance that the bandits would take that option, or another, before too long. Sooner or later it would not matter whether he gave them the information they wanted - especially since he really did not know anything. He was a liability, and they would be done with him.

He only prayed that Ravi had found out something that would help with their escape, because he had nothing.

17

AMBUSH

Raedrick squinted his eyes against the glare of the sunlight reflecting off the snow on the slope in front of them and considered the way ahead. The trail led upwards and to the right, veering around the base of a sheer cliff that stretched upward for several hundred feet. The base was riddled with fallen boulders and the cliff face itself was riven by large vertical cracks, all custom-made hiding spots, should someone wish to conceal himself.

It was the perfect place for an ambush.

He looked sidelong at Povol, who had stopped a few feet to his left and stood waiting calmly. The mountaineer had not found the climb up-slope difficult at all. He showed no signs of sweat or fatigue; his breathing was slow and regular. Whereas Raedrick felt like a raw recruit, unable to handle a run of more than a mile, sucking down air like it would run out in the next minute. Of course, Povol made a living by prowling these mountains all year round, in all conditions. Raedrick's own job was…less strenuous. Most days.

That did not make him feel particularly better about himself.

"You think they're waiting for us up there." It was not a question.

Raedrick considered for a moment, then nodded. That was where *he* would post a rear guard.

But then, they had passed several places during their pursuit that would have been ideal ambush sites, and always found nothing. Maybe this Geoff was not as clever as Raedrick had given him credit for. Maybe.

"Makes sense. Lots of good chimneys in that face. Lots of nooks and crannies. Plenty of places to hide, if you have the hankering."

Raedrick nodded again.

Povol waited for a several seconds before speaking again. "So, we going ahead or not?"

Of course they were going ahead. That was not a question. Not for Raedrick. And after the loss of his dogs, not for Povol either.

Raedrick had found it strange, at first, that the dogs' fate would move the man so, where the fate of human beings he knew and associated with on a near-daily basis apparently did not. He understood Povol's grief: the dogs had been his friends, maybe even his family. But they were still only dogs.

After last night he knew better than to tell Povol that, though.

The had followed the trail, Raedrick leading the way with his borrowed longsword in hand, at the ready. They marched for hours; he pushed on through the ever-deepening darkness, easily picking out the obvious signs of the brigands' passing despite the dark. Every moment, he expected to meet an attack from the rear-guard. But always there was none.

Eventually, despite Raedrick's fiercest urgings to himself, fatigue began to get the better of him. His vision blurred to the point that he could not see where he was going. Or maybe the moon set and the darkness of night truly set in. Regardless, he was forced to admit they could not go on, not and expect to do any good while doing so.

Looking at Povol, for a moment he feared he had already waited too long. But after Raedrick managed to get a fire going, carefully hidden from prying eyes behind a small thicket and a pit dug into the snow and earth around the place he put the campfire, Povol came back around rather quickly.

The two men sat beside the fire, scooting as close as they dared to heat as much of themselves up as possible. For a while, they sat in silence until finally Povol spoke, softly.

"Never had many friends."

Raedrick poked at the fire with a stick, sending a stream of glowing sparks skyward as the fuel shifted. He looked at Povol sidelong. "Come again?"

The mountaineer just shrugged. "Me and other people don't really see eye to eye, for the most part." He smirked slightly. "You might have noticed."

Raedrick had noticed; tales of the man's many fights were hard to ignore. But he did not press the point.

Povol sighed, never taking his eyes off the heart of the flame. "Never had any family, growing up. Guess that's what caused it. But the dogs, though... They never mocked me, never let me down." He shook himself and forced his eyes away from the flame. His eyes met Raedrick's, and Raedrick could not deny the pain and loss the man felt. "I first started in the mountains because of the dogs, you know. If it weren't for them..." He sighed and looked down at the dirt and snow at his feet.

There was something about the way he looked, hunched over like that, that raised the hackles of Raedrick's neck. "What?"

Povol was silent for almost a full minute. When he spoke, it was so low as to be almost inaudible. "I had thought for months about ending it. I just that week came up with the perfect plan. I would tie a big rock around my ankles and jump off the end of one of the docks." He voice caught. Raedrick saw tears well up, but Povol held up a restraining hand, and Raedrick kept still. The mountaineer drew a deep breath. "But then one morning, my sled team finally meshed. We executed the most difficult maneuver in the repertoire flawlessly." He laughed quietly. "It was the very morning I was planning to jump. But when I got back from my morning rounds and unclipped the dogs, they seemed to know how much a milestone we had just passed. They yipped and jumped, bounded all around me. And looking at them..."

"You realized you couldn't do it."

Povol shook his head. "I realized I didn't *want* to do it."

Raedrick did not know how to respond to that at first. He had never been particularly fond of dogs himself, and though did not want to belittle Povol's obviously profound experience, he could not relate. Then again, it was clear that one morning changed Povol's life forever, and turned his dogs from just friends to family, a family far more enduring, more special than any he had known up until then.

Maybe that was not so strange, after all.

Raedrick shook himself back to the present, leaving memories of last night behind. Drawing his sword again, he gave Povol a serious look. "When they come, it will be from both sides at once. There will probably be three or four of them. If they're smart, they'll use bows so we can't get close. If not..." He shrugged. "If not, we may have a chance."

Povol scowled at him in response. "You're saying we can't win."

"Ambushes are designed to make it that way."

"So we're going forward...why?"

Raedrick grinned at him. "Because the best way to mess up an ambush is to trigger it."

He hustled up the slope, making a brisk pace but being careful not to go too fast. He did not want to tire himself too much before the fighting started.

Behind him, he heard Povol curse and mutter, "That doesn't make any sense at all." But he followed. That was the important part.

They were only two, and they hid themselves exactly where Raedrick thought they would have. No imagination, and less thought. Taking them down was far easier than he would have hoped.

He rounded the large boulder and immediately dove to his left, tucking his shoulder into a roll and springing up onto his feet just as the first of them emerged from the crack in the cliff face where he had been hiding. The surprise on the man's face when his presumptive prey went from where it was supposed to be - an easy kill - to right in his face was classic.

Raedrick almost felt sorry for him as he thrust the tip of his borrowed longsword at his gut, and that almost cost him his head.

The bandit was surprised, but still well-trained. He hopped backwards, sweeping his own sword in a downward arc that knocked Raedrick's blade aside, then he followed up with a back-handed cut toward Raedrick's throat. Only the bandit's backward momentum saved him; the blade whistled past, maybe an inch from Raedrick's flesh.

The counter left the bandit open, and Raedrick wasted no time in pressing forward, inside the reach of the man's sword, and thrusting up with his own weapon.

The man jerked once when Raedrick's sword entered his chest, right at the point where the ribs meet. Then he went limp and slid slowly to the ground.

A cry of pain made him spin around in time to see the second bandit go down, Povol's spear buried deeply into his side.

Guess that answered the question of Povol's readiness and ability to fight with his strong hand injured and barely usable.

Raedrick exchanged a victorious grin with the mountaineer, and only then did it register just how close that encounter had come to ending him. The heat of exertion was replaced by a chill that went right to his bones, and he shivered. No matter how many battles he fought in, he never had managed to shake the after action let-down, the terror that sprang up from having faced death and survived, somehow.

Povol wrenched his spear free and gave Raedrick a strange look. "You alright?"

Raedrick drew a deep breath and nodded, making a dismissive gesture with his free hand. "Fine." He peered more closely at the mountaineer. "You?"

Povol shrugged, saying nothing.

That was either good or very bad. You never could tell how a man would react to battle. Some panic or freeze up, some come through without an issue. And some come to revel in the bloodshed.

"It is a hard thing," Raedrick began.

But Povol cut him off with a snort. "Ain't my first time in a fight, Constable." He smirked, derisively. "I'm not some tenderfoot that needs handholding."

Raedrick supposed that was fair enough. "Alright. Let's see to the bodies and get moving."

❧ 18 ❧

LATE NIGHT VISITOR

Julian awoke with a start. It was still dark; he could see only varying degrees of shadow within the little tent, but his nose told him another person was with him. That, and a looming sense of presence. His skin tingled with apprehension for a moment as all manner of possibilities ran through his mind as to what his visitor wanted.

"Julian." It was Ravi's voice, speaking just barely above a whisper.

Relief flooded through him and he let out the breath he was holding. The shadows shifted, accompanied by the sound of rustling clothing, then Ravi spoke again, closer to his ear.

"We have to get you out of here." He paused, and Julian heard him swallow. "They thought I was asleep, but I overheard them talking. The men they left to bring up the rear never returned. The others met with Geoff, and…"

He did not have to say the rest. They had to know it was Raedrick, and maybe Povol, who took out their rearguard. With enemies coming up the rear, the last thing they would need was someone slowing them down, or betraying their presence.

But on the other hand, he could be a useful hostage…

No. No, they had Ravi for that. And by his oaths as a

guildsman he would do them no harm. He might refuse to treat them if they tried to force him, but he would not harm them. The brigands could not count on Julian to do that.

That left only one answer as to what to do with him.

"When?"

"First thing in the morning."

Julian licked his lips, but his mouth had suddenly gone dry. "Ok," he said, "what's the plan?"

"I found a knife," Ravi said, his voice trembled slightly, and he sounded uncertain. "I think I can cut you free."

Julian nodded, though he knew Ravi would not be able to see it. "Get started."

Ravi moved again in the darkness, and Julian felt the old man's hands on his chest, feeling around where the straps crossed his body and attached to the bedding beneath him. It was actually a fairly clever piece of work, when he thought about it. If…

Wait a minute.

"Ravi, how did you get in here?"

"What do you…" Ravi trailed off, the dismay in his tone making it clear that he saw it too.

Why had the bandits left his tent unguarded? There had always been a guard on Julian the entire time he had been there. And, for that matter, on Ravi as well.

Ravi froze. "Should I…?"

Julian shook his head vigorously. The die was cast. The only way was forward. "Do it," he said. "Quickly."

The old man's hands resumed their groping in the darkness for what seemed hours. In reality it was only a few seconds, tops. But at the end, after several strong tugs and more than one painful poke when Ravi slipped with his knife - Julian hoped it did not draw too much blood, but right then blood loss was the least of his concerns - the pressure on his chest let up and then fell away altogether.

"I think I got it," Ravi said.

Julian took a deep breath and tried to sit up, trying not to hope that the old man was right.

The relief he felt when he rose, unimpeded, bordered on ecstasy. "Yes!" he said as loudly as he dared, exulting in his newfound freedom of movement. "Well done, Ravi." He rolled his shoulders and twisted his torso back and forth to work out the kinks. It was as comfortable as rolling over gravel.

No time to gripe about it, though. "Help me up," he said, and found Ravi's hand. Holding on to the old man, he forced himself to his feet. There he stood wavering for a few seconds while he found his equilibrium.

If he remembered right, Geoff had his tent in the center of the camp, with the others arranged in a ring surrounding his. Very much like the patterns Julian had used during his time in the Army. Not for the first time, he pondered whether Geoff and his men were deserters. It seemed likely, from how they acted.

Hard to hold that against them, all things considered. Julian was not *that* much of a hypocrite.

"I think there is one man on watch," Ravi said quietly. "I heard him walking around out there."

Julian nodded. It made sense. Without the two men they left as rearguard, there were only seven of the bandits remaining. Putting two men on watch at a time would mean three shifts, since Julian would bet his next ten paydays Geoff was not going to stand any watch. That would leave them all strung out on not enough sleep, as opposed to just a few of them.

Come to think of it, that was probably why there was no guard at his tent, as well. Not like he was going anywhere.

One sentry ought not be too difficult to avoid.

"Ok, let's go. Keep low and stay in the shadows. We'll head out the side of the camp opposite the sentry, then double back to the trail. We keep going until we meet up with Rae and Povol, and then we get ourselves back to town, quick as we can."

"And just leave these criminals to their business?"

Julian paused. He found that idea troublesome as well, but

they were not exactly in the position to take up a crusade for justice here. "Way I see it, we would not have known about these guys at all if Tolburt hadn't come to town. They weren't out here hurting anyone but him." He scowled in the darkness. "And that, they are welcome to do."

With that, he parted the flaps of his tent and looked outside.

19

ESCAPE

The camp was arranged as Julian recalled: a clustering of small tents surrounding a larger tent in the center. A communal fire smoldered in its pit outside the entrance flaps to Geoff's tent, the coals giving off a dull red glow as they cooled. The smell of woodsmoke and burned meat hung in the air, and soft snores issued from several of the tents.

It was a restful sight, as long as one did not know who the camp's inhabitants were.

Julian slipped out of his tent and around the corner, crouching in the shadows between his tent and the next. And boy did that make his thighs scream in protest.

Ravi came close on his heels, still clutching his knife in a trembling hand.

Julian reached out his hand to the old man. "Let me take that."

Ravi blinked, then after a second, nodded understanding and passed the knife over. Its weight, though slight, brought Julian a bit of reassurance. At least he was not completely unarmed, although he held no illusions about his chances if he had to face one of the bandits, armed as they were.

"I need to get a sword," he mumbled.

Ravi frowned at him and opened his mouth to speak.

The sound of two rocks striking together from behind them and to the left stopped Ravi's words. Julian turned to look that way, but only saw the shadows of night. He held his breath, waiting and watching.

Another sound, softer than before but still noticeable, issued from the darkness. Then again.

A man walking through the snow. He was being careful about it, but there was only so much one could do to be silent in conditions like this; snow and ice will crunch underfoot, whatever you do.

It was the sentry. It had to be.

An idea sprung to Julian's mind. It was risky, very risky. If he botched it, the entire camp would know what was going on, and then they would be finished. But if he pulled it off...

He needed a sword. It was worth the risk.

"Wait here," he whispered to Ravi, who blinked in surprise. A moment later, his eyes widened, and he gave a vigorous shake of his head. Julian raised a finger to his lips. No time for arguments.

Then he set off into the darkness, toward the sentry.

Stepping out of the ring of tents, Julian took a moment to let his eyes adjust to the deeper darkness. It came as a bit of a surprise that the deeper darkness really was not all that deep. The ground was blanketed in snow, except where protruding rocks had been cleared by the wind, and between the stars and the glow on the western horizon that announced the moon's imminent rise there was a bit of light for the snow to reflect. So after only a very short time, Julian found he could see passing well.

The light was good enough for him to see the sentry, a dark spot against the slightly brighter background of snow, moving away from him, about thirty feet off.

Julian took a deep breath to calm himself and flexed his fingers on the hilt of Ravi's knife. He was already beginning to feel the chill; the bandits had taken most of his outer garments when they tied him and left him in the tent. Another reason they did not bother with a guard. And yet another reason that he had to risk doing this. Now that he was out of the shelter provided by the cluster of tents, Julian felt certain he would not be able to make it down the mountain without some more layers.

Moving as quickly as he dared, he pushed through the snow until he reached the sentry's footprints. He took a step, and grinned. The sentry's stride was about the same length as his.

This was working out better than he had hoped.

He moved forward, stepping from footprint to footprint and being careful not to punch through the snow any place else - that was the sound that he had heard from back by the tent, and he did not want to risk giving himself away.

Which was not exactly a way to walk quickly. Fortunately, the sentry was not exactly brisk in his movements either, and Julian gained ground fairly rapidly.

Of course, it would only take the sentry turning around, and the gig would be up.

Twenty feet.

How could this guy be so stupid that he had not even stopped walking, or checked his rear, at all?

Cursing himself for questioning his good fortune, Julian picked up the pace.

Ten feet, and the sentry stopped.

Julian tried to stop as well, but he stumbled forward and ended up crunching through the snow right behind the man.

"What the - " the sentry began, turning around.

Their eyes met, and the sentry's widened in shock. He reached for his sword.

Idiot should have called out. Julian hurtled forward, slamming bodily into the man and forcing his sword arm into his torso. They went down, and Julian grabbed the back of the man's neck with his left hand and stabbed upward with the dagger in his right.

Only then did the man think to cry out, but it was too late. He only got out a short shout before the knife sliced through his Adam's Apple.

The man squirmed, rolling the two of them over. Julian worked hard to keep his grip on the knife, then continued the roll, bringing himself up on top of the sentry.

Growling a curse, he put all his weight onto the knife's hilt. The blade crunched against something solid, and the man spasmed.

Then he lay still.

Julian rolled off of the body and lay panting for a long moment. It had only been a short burst of activity, but it had drained him completely.

Price you pay for a couple days of torture, forced marching, bad sleep, and almost no food.

Finally he pushed himself up to a sitting position and took a look at the dead bandit.

He was dressed as they all were: in furs and wools, though the furs had been augmented recently, by Povol's dogs if memory served. Julian would not be taking those, and not just because, uncured as they were, they had begun to stink.

The rest, though, was fair game.

Julian worked quickly, unbuckling the fellow's sword belt and pulling off his outer layers, then donning them himself. Finally, he strapped the sword on and cinched the belt tight.

Good to go.

He took one last look down at the fallen sentry, and suddenly realized who it was. Stefan.

Julian felt his eyebrows climb high on his forehead. If he had…

He squatted down and patted the man down. Sure enough, there, tucked into a pocket of his breaches - Julian had not bothered with them before - he found that piece of paper Stefan had been consulting all day. He unfolded it carefully and held it up, so the reflected light of the stars could illuminate it a bit better.

He could not see much, but it looked like a map.

Julian grinned from ear to ear.

Ravi shivered, and not just from the cold. He had not been this nervous, frightened really, in years. His position as a guildsman of the Healers Circle had functioned better than any suit of armor, shielding him from potential harm, and he had taken it for granted.

But here, now, doing this... This was different. His status would offer no protection from Geoff and his men if they learned what he had done this night.

Although truth be told he was not sure how much protection it really would have offered him anyway. This bunch seemed like the types to get rid of anyone who was of no more use. They had done it already, with Tolburt and now Julian. What was to say Ravi would not be next?

That did not make this evening's deeds any easier to deal with.

His eyes darted around from tent to tent. He imagined that at any moment Geoff's men would come storming out, wise to what he had done, and string him up, and Julian with him. Every minute that passed without that happening seemed an eternity, and a miracle.

At one point, he heard a noise from outside the circle of tents, almost like a man's shout, but muffled, cut off too quickly. He stiffened, pressing himself against the side of Julian's old tent, his heart suddenly pounding in his ears. If he had heard that, surely one of the men in the tents would have as well. It must have roused one of them from his slumber, and he would be out to investigate, and then they would be caught.

Oh Gods, why did he get himself into this? He could have sent young Willam. He was more than up to the task. But no, Ravi the foolish had to go off on an adventure, because he was bored. Stupid old fool.

What are you saying? Better Willam than you?

Chastened, Ravi forced his thoughts back into order. He was no coward; he would not wish his troubles off onto someone else, especially not a fine young man like Willam.

No, he would see this through. And when he got back…

If you get back.

When he got back, he would have a big pot of tea and never again dream of going off on an exciting adventure. He was far too old for this sort of thing.

"Ravi."

The voice, coming from the dark night behind him, made him jump. He almost cried a surrender, hoping against hope that they would still honor his protected status.

"Ravi, come on."

He recognized the voice. Julian. Ravi breathed out a sigh of relief, then crept out into the darkness to meet him.

It was time to go.

20

REUNION

Raedrick and Povol spent an extremely uncomfortable night crammed between two spurs of rock, with the nighttime winds howling all around. There was little rest to be had, at least not for Raedrick's part. Between the bitter cold and Povol's far too close proximity - the man truly did stink, though Raedrick was willing to admit he probably did as well - he only managed to doze on and off most of the night.

At least it was a clear night, and the stars shown brightly. That made Raedrick's interminable wakefulness not completely unbearable.

It was with a fuzzy head, a growing headache, and a gnawing belly that he set off further up the mountain the next morning.

"Wish there was some game," Povol said at one point as they trudged onwards.

Raedrick was inclined to agree. The two brigands who tried to ambush them had only a meal's worth of supplies on them. It was the first food he or Povol had eaten in a day, and it did not go far toward relieving their hunger. And that was yesterday afternoon.

It was going to be a very long, very uncomfortable day.

Raedrick had almost become used to the glare of the sun off the white snow, pristine save for the tracks of the passing brigands and their captives. Even still, Povol put him to shame a couple hours later.

"Someone's coming," he said, pointing his spear toward the trail ahead.

Raedrick squinted, trying to see through the glare. He could barely make out two forms walking toward them. Just barely. How in the hell did Povol do that?

He looked around for cover, but they were well out onto the snowpack. The closest thing approaching concealment was a small depression about fifty feet to their right.

Povol must have noticed him looking around, because he shook his head. "They've got the sun in their eyes, but they'll see us any minute now, if they haven't already."

Raedrick nodded. He had pretty much figured that out himself. But it was good to hear the expert say it, all the same. Or a least that was what he told himself.

"Spread out, and be ready for a fight."

Povol shrugged and took a couple steps to his left, taking hold of his spear in both hands, though he carried it the way a left-handed man would. Raedrick noted he still was only able to lightly close the fingers of his right hand around the haft. That would be a serious disadvantage in a fight.

Then again, just yesterday he had proved more than capable of overcoming that disadvantage, so maybe Raedrick was just picking nits for the sake of having something to worry about.

He snorted at that thought, drawing his longsword and taking a step to his right.

Then he settled down to wait.

The two men ahead spread out, lowering into ready crouches and brandishing their weapons. Any other time, that would make Julian nervous. But with this pair? A spear and a longsword. An awkwardly-wielded longsword at that. That could only be Raedrick and Povol.

He kept his weapon sheathed and picked up his pace, grinning broadly.

"I would have thought you'd be more happy to see us, Rae," he shouted, when he and Ravi were close enough.

The effect on the two men was most satisfying. Raedrick gave a little jerk and straightened, leaning forward slightly as though trying to see them better. Povol...

Povol snorted and spat onto the snow at his feet, then straightened and raised his spear, resting it over his left shoulder. "Thought sure you'd be dead by now," he called, earning a reproachful look from Raedrick. Povol returned the look and shrugged. "What? It's true."

Raedrick slipped his sword back into place behind his belt - he did not have a scabbard - and hurried across the distance between himself and Julian, smiling in what appeared to be a mixture of relief and joy. They clasped hands and Julian returned the grin.

"How did you get away from them?"

Julian shrugged and gestured toward Ravi. "All his doing."

Ravi smiled sheepishly. "It was nothing. Truly." But the twinkle in his eyes told another tale completely.

Raedrick clasped hands with the old man, and Povol gave him a respectful nod.

"Well," Julian said, "Let's get on home."

Raedrick frowned, peering back up the slope and the bandits' trail. "How many remain?"

"Six," Julian said with resignation. He had been afraid of this; Raedrick was about to get obstinate. Julian dug into his pocket and produced the map, "I took care of Tolburt's little buddy. Look what I found."

Raedrick took the map and unfolded it. One eyebrow rose as he looked it over, then he gazed at Julian questioningly.

"Those guys are out of luck without that," Julian said. "I'll bet you a mark against a penny they're here for that treasure Tolburt talked about, and that's the map to it."

Povol perked up noticeably. "Never heard of buried treasure in these parts."

Julian shrugged. "Me neither, but that's the story."

Raedrick handed Povol the map, and the mountaineer began looking it over. All of a sudden, Raedrick had one of those expressions on his face that told Julian he was about to volunteer them for something stupid, and dangerous.

"What are you thinking, Rae?"

Raedrick pursed his lips. "They will still cause trouble out here, map or no."

Julian shook his head. "That treasure - if it even exists - is the only reason they're here. Without a way to reach it, they'll fold up tents and go home. Or turn on each other and take care the problem for us."

Raedrick gave him a level look. "Do you really believe that, Julian?"

Julian frowned, hating where Raedrick was going with this one. He wanted to believe what he had just said. But he had to admit it was just as likely Geoff and his men would choose the other path, the one that involved becoming enraged, following them back to Lydelton, and wreaking havoc.

But hang it all, the four of them were neither equipped nor prepared to deal with that bunch out here. At the least, they needed to get back to town, resupply, and get a few more strong backs at their side. He had heard Gilroy and the other fishing men who fought against Isenholf's band last spring bragging over their mugs on many a night. At least a couple of them, or barring that dozens of other local men who had not participated and now wished they had, would likely stand up to help take down Geoff and his bunch. There were only six of them, after all.

He opened his mouth to say all this, but right then Povol erupted with laughter. All eyes went to the mountaineer, who was slapping his thigh with glee.

"Povol?" Ravi said, carefully.

Povol looked up from the map wearing the biggest smirk of amusement Julian had ever seen, and he had seen plenty. "Bloody fools went the wrong way!"

Julian blinked, confused. He exchanged glances with Raedrick, who did not look much better. "Come again?"

Povol shook his head and held up the map so they could all see. "See here? This is Tollard's Peak. And this," he pointed on the map to another mountain to the northeast that sat right up against the Northflow, "this is that mountain over there." He pointed away from the map, toward a smaller ridge off to the east.

Julian looked at the peak, but it just looked like one more mountain to him. "Are you sure?"

Povol glared at him. "I'm been roaming these mountains longer than you've been chasing skirts. I'm telling you, that's the mountain from the map. Look." He jabbed his finger at the peak. "See the river running past it, to the north?"

Julian squinted. He could just barely see a dark squiggle running to the north, past the mountain. He shrugged. "Guess so."

"That's what it is." Povol shook his head. "Those fools have been slowly veering north for the last day and a half. They climbed the wrong damn mountain!" He spat into the snow. "If they'd bothered to hire a guide, someone who knows the land, they'd have gotten to their precious treasure already."

"And that guide would likely be dead," Ravi said, solemnly.

That took some of the fire out of Povol. He paused, shut his mouth, then nodded, looking down at the ground. "Yeah."

"That's very interesting. Let's get moving home."

"Julian."

"No, Rae." Julian wagged a finger at his friend. "We need food, weapons, and people if we want to take on these guys and win. We don't have any of it." Well, they did. Sort of. "Ok, not enough of it. If you want to come back and find this treasure later, fine. But…"

"It's actually on the way," Povol interjected.

Damn him. "What do you mean? No it isn't."

"Well," Povol pointed back down the slope they stood on, and toward Tollard's Peak. "We could head back down into the valley, then up Tollard's Peak, then back down again. Or," he swept his hand around to point due east, toward the southern slope of the little mountain next to the river, "we could descend this way, cut across the lower portion of that mountain, and follow the North-flow to the lake."

"I thought you said it runs through a gorge and we couldn't walk it, when we came up here," Ravi said.

Povol nodded. "It does. But I happen to know a hunting lodge not far from the base of that mountain. Folks keep it stocked with supplies and have a couple canoes tied up, to use for paddling upstream."

Crap. That solved half of Julian's objections right there.

Raedrick nodded. "I think that takes care of that." He turned to give Julian a grin that was just a bit too smug. "Don't you?"

Julian sighed. He could probably think of more problems with this plan, but he was out-voted and he knew it. He nodded, conceding defeat. "How long to get there?"

Povol squinted up at the sun for a second then shrugged. "A bit after sunset, if we're lucky."

"Well then," Raedrick said. "Let's be off."

21

RIVER LODGE

Night was fully upon them by the time they reached the lodge, and with it cold that rivaled any they had encountered so far on this venture. Several times, Raedrick thought they might have to stop early, so bitter the night was. But there was no place that looked appealing, or even promising. Oh, there were rocks and cracks in the sides of the slope, a thicket or two once they got back down into the tree-filled valley, and once a collection of fallen logs that lay over a gully, but after the previous night, he did not relish the notion of stopping in any of those places.

Neither did anyone else, or at least no one suggested a stop. He supposed the notion of spending the night indoors with a fire fueled them as much as it did him.

He almost did not see the lodge when they arrived. In the dark, it looked like a particularly large boulder, or a bushy tree. But as they drew near, the straight lines of the structure became more clear and they were able to behold the goal of their trek.

It could more appropriately be called a shack. It stood on stilts about five feet tall and appeared roughly constructed of hewn logs that were probably sealed with mud. It had no windows, just a small chimney rising from the thatched roof.

Raedrick had seen worse hovels, but this one came close. Maybe it would look more welcoming in the daylight, but he doubted it.

"Why the stilts?" Julian asked as they approached.

"During the spring thaw, the river runs pretty high up here," Povol said. "The place flooded out a few times before we decided to raise it up."

That made sense.

The door to the lodge was locked, naturally, but that proved no difficulty, as Povol produced a key from one of his pockets.

They stepped inside and Povol lit a lamp that hung from a hook on the wall to the right.

The lamp's soft glow illuminated a well-stocked and orderly place, much nicer than Raedrick would have thought based on the exterior. The lodge was a single room, with three sets of bunk beds along the rear wall. Off to the left, a stone fireplace dominated the wall, with half a cord of split wood stacked neatly in a cast iron bin next to it. A simple wooden table, flanked by a pair of benches, sat in the center of the room. The right-hand wall was dominated by a long counter, which held a collection of tableware and two tapped casks. Cabinets below the counter no doubt held all manner of supplies, if Povol could be believed. The entire place smelled pleasantly of wood, woodsmoke, and some manner of incense or other. All told, it was a more than passable place to hole up.

"Nice," Julian said, approvingly. He wasted no time in heading to the fireplace.

"Who owns this place, Povol?" Ravi asked.

Povol closed the door, shutting out the wind. The place seemed strangely silent, and Raedrick suddenly realized just how used to the constant whistling of the wind he had become. It almost seemed unnatural to not have it in his ears.

"It's not owned by any one person," Povol said as he walked over to the counter and picked up a mug. "A bunch of us who drink at Holb's chip in to maintain it. Holb manages the till and makes sure everyone pays their due." He opened the tap on the nearest cask, and amber fluid flowed into his mug for a moment. Shutting the tap, he turned to the rest of them and took a swig. His contented sigh as he lowered the mug spoke volumes. "Mead, boys?"

Raedrick could not help but grin in response.

Ten minutes later, everything was just a bit brighter. Julian got the fire going. Ravi found dried fruits and meat in the cupboards, and Povol poured them all a round from the cask. They sat around the table in a state of warm contentment, and right then it was easy to forget about their problems.

Of course, that could not last.

"Do you think they're following us, Constable?" Ravi asked. He had only sipped at his mead but already he looked flushed, as though the drink was going right to his head.

Povol snorted and took a long draw from his mug. "They'd have to be blind to miss our trail. I'd be after us if I was them." His eyes narrowed and he added, "Sooner the better," in a dark tone. The good cheer he expressed earlier was gone, replaced by a hard scowl that spoke to his anger and loss more than his words could have.

Raedrick exchanged looks with Julian, who was watching Povol carefully. "Best if we can avoid any more contact with them," Raedrick said slowly. "There's been enough blood spilled."

Ravi nodded emphatic agreement.

Povol just snorted again.

Silence settled around them, the cheery mood broken, and they sat for a time just drinking and thinking. After a few minutes, Povol stood, mug in hand, and turned toward the cask. That would not do.

"Keep it to just one, Povol. We need to keep our wits about us."

The mountaineer stared at Raedrick for a moment, his scowl darkening. Then, with a sigh, he nodded. Instead of the tapped cask, he strode to another barrel that stood near the fireplace and opened the lid. He stood there for a few seconds, scowling. "Still frozen."

Well, that was hardly a shock. The water in the barrel was likely frozen solid from the weeks of winter before they had arrived. An hour near a fire would not make up for that. Raedrick though about making a run to the river with a bucket, but that would be treacherous in the dark; it could wait until morning, and then they would be off anyway.

Povol suddenly smacked his right hand down into the barrel, his fist curled into a hammer. Or mostly curled; it was hard to see under his bandages. A solid thump as his hand struck the solid ice preceded a loud curse form the mountaineer by a second or so. He dropped his mug and cradled his injured hand against his chest, drawing in deep breaths in through his nose while he clenched his teeth. His face was a rictus of pain.

Ravi was on his feet in an instant. "Povol, what are you doing?" He rushed over to the mountaineer, reaching out toward his injury.

Povol pushed him away with his good hand and a fierce glare.

But Ravi would not be dissuaded. "Let me have a look at it," he said, his tone insistent, forceful. He and Povol locked eyes for a few seconds. Then, finally, the mountaineer looked down and nodded.

Ravi led him back to the table and bad him sit. Then he gently took Povol's hand and unwrapped the bandage. The mountaineer winced at every turn of the cloth.

Ravi unwrapped the last layer of bandage and his breath caught. His eyes widened in alarm, flicking from the wound to Raedrick and back. "Oh. This..." He licked his lips, concern written all over his face. "This is not good."

Raedrick stood so he could get a better look, and almost immediately wished he had not.

Povol's hand was swollen and discolored. In the immediate area of the wound, it was almost red, fading to a dull pink at his wrist and fingers. The wound no longer bled, but it oozed a yellowish puss, and there was an unpleasant odor. Raedrick had smelled that before; the smell of infection.

"Son of a bitch," Raedrick breathed.

Povol just scowled, his brow furrowed, and Raedrick realized that what he had taken as anger for much of the last couple days was mostly pain. In must have been maddening, but Povol hardly let on to it. Tough fellow.

And stupid. If he had told someone earlier, they could have… What? There was nothing to be done, not out here.

"Is it…" Julian did not finish the thought, but Raedrick knew they were all thinking it. Is the hand savable?

Ravi frowned, turning Povol's hand over to look at the other side of the puncture. "Can you move the fingers at all?"

The mountaineer shrugged and tried. All five fingers moved, but only a little, and Raedrick could tell it was only with great difficulty and pain.

"What do you think?" Raedrick asked the guildsman.

Ravi shook his head. "It is badly infected. I had medicines and ointments that may have been able to help, but Geoff's men took them when they captured us. There are more back at the guild house. But…" He looked from the hand to Povol's face, his expression pitying. "If we don't get to them soon, I'm afraid it'll have to be amputated."

"Crap," Julian said. He stood and pulled his coat back on, along with his gloves and hat. "The canoes are stored under the lodge, right?"

Povol nodded. "In racks."

Julian nodded. "I'll go check and make sure they're still there, then we're getting you out of here at first light."

"No."

Julian stopped halfway to the door and looked back at Povol, surprise and consternation competing on his face.

Raedrick concurred. "Povol, this is serious."

Povol looked at all three of them challengingly, his scowl

renewed in its forcefulness. "Damn right it is. Those bastards took my dogs, and I'm not…"

Ravi broke in, his voice gentle but firm. "Do you want them to take your hand as well?"

Povol just glowered in silence.

"Because that's what will happen if you remain out here."

The mountaineer looked down at his injured hand and his stubborn scowl faded, replaced by acceptance. He sighed, but it was more a groan. Then he nodded.

22

EVACUATION

First light came sooner than Raedrick's body would have liked. It seemed he had only just closed his eyes when Julian was shaking him awake. He blinked away the sleep, fighting off the urge to just lie back, shut his eyes, and get a few more minutes of rest. Just a few more minutes.

With a grunt, he forced himself to sit up, only remembering that the ceiling was low above the top bunk where he lay when he hit his forehead on one of the ceiling timbers. That knocked the sleepiness right out of him.

"They just put that there," Julian quipped as Raedrick clutched at the swiftly-growing lump, but from his tone his heart was not in the jibe.

Who could blame him. A hard day lay before them. Even harder than Julian knew.

By the time he managed to get past the ache in his head, chomp down some dried breakfast, and get his gear squared away, the other men were already clothed and mustered outside. Raedrick felt like one of the walking dead as he clumped down the stairs from the door, but they did not look much better - especially Povol - so there was no sense complaining about it.

"The canoes are in the water, ready to go, Rae," Julian reported.

Raedrick nodded. "The river gets fairly rough in places, or so I've heard." He looked at Povol, questioningly.

The mountaineer shrugged. He looked decidedly pale this morning. "In the spring, it will. These days it's mostly frozen except for the middle and the water's low. Shouldn't be too hard."

Raedrick nodded again. He did not need to order them to make haste.

There were racks for four canoes between the stilts that held the lodge aloft, but as they trooped toward the river, Raedrick could see two of them were empty. He presumed Julian had taken those two for the group's use. A dozen paces later, they pushed through undergrowth that was little more than bare twigs and branches and came to a small inlet that was separated from the river proper by a series of boulders that looked as though they had been rolled into place by some great giant's design, so well did they create the sheltered cove.

It was frozen over now, of course, but Raedrick could see in his mind's eye how the area would look in the middle of summer: all green undergrowth, with flowers interspersed here and there, birds alighting in the trees that in places grew right up to the water's edge, and the cove itself calm and flat like a mirror reflecting the beauty around it. It was easy to tell why the outdoorsmen had chosen this place to build their lodge.

There was just one thing wrong.

"Where are the canoes?" Ravi spoke the question before Raedrick could.

Julian smirked bemusedly at the guildsman. "Can't really put them in here, can we?" He gestured for them to follow, them set off around the boulders, moving quickly but carefully down a beaten path in the snow, where he had clearly gone before.

It only took a moment to round the rocks, and Raedrick beheld the Northflow itself. The river was more narrow than he thought it would be. Down where it joined with Lake Glimmermere, the

Northflow was well over a hundred yards across, but it was very shallow, even away from the ford. Here, it was maybe a hundred feet from shore to shore. Thinking about it for a moment, though, it made sense. The river was probably deeper here. Or something.

As Povol predicted, the river was frozen over except for a portion about twenty feet wide in its center, where the current was great enough to prevent the ice from growing any further. The canoes were, true to Julian's word, in the water, but nestled in a hollow of broken-out ice that allowed the current to eddy around without carrying the boats away.

Raedrick frowned; that hollow was not natural. He cast an accusatory gaze at Julian. "You should have woken me to help you."

Povol snorted out a half-laugh. "Tried to," he said. "Julian practically shook the teeth out of your head, but you did not stir a whit."

Raedrick blinked. That never happened; he was a very light sleeper. Always had been.

"Guess you were pretty tired," Julian said, grinning at him teasingly. Then he shrugged. "It's ok, Povol and me managed it without too much trouble."

Raedrick rather doubted that, but there was no point grousing over it.

They carefully walked out across the ice to where the boats lay waiting. It was a disquieting experience, actually. Sure, Raedrick had been out on Lake Glimmermere a time or two, at Lani's insistence every time, and he knew that Julian and Povol had been out here earlier, so there was every reason to believe the ice was more than sufficient to hold them. All the same, the thought of all that icy cold just beneath his feet, and the knowledge of exactly how little time he could survive in it, sent preemptive shivers up his spine.

Finally they reached the boats.

"Are you good with a canoe, Ravi?"

The guildsman gave a little shrug. "I paddled a little, in my youth." That was not saying much, but the confident smile on his lips as he replied belied the humble words.

"That makes one of us," Julian said.

There was no need to ask Povol about his skill level. He was likely better in a boat than any of them, but he could not paddle, not with his hand injured.

"Alright." Raedrick pulled out the map Julian had retrieved from Stefan and unfolded it. "Let's see. Povol, correct me if I'm wrong, but we're right here."

He pointed at where he presumed the lodge to be, and the mountaineer nodded. "Thereabouts, yes."

Raedrick nodded, the possibilities churning in his head. It would be a relatively quick trip down river to the lake, but a longer walk back to town; they would not be able to paddle the whole way, not with the lake frozen over as it was. But there was no reason to expect any major difficulties, and they ought to have Povol to the Healers Circle well before nightfall.

But there was that other matter.

"What about this?" He pointed upstream, toward where the spot marking the treasure was inked, and looked Povol in the eye.

The mountaineer blinked in surprise. "I'd say it's just a couple miles upstream. Why?"

"Rae, what are you doing? We have to get Povol back to town." He could just about feel Julian's accusing stare boring through his head.

Raedrick drew in a deep breath and nodded to himself, the decision made. "And you will."

Julian's eyes widened, and he shook his head emphatically. "No, Rae. We're all going if -"

He cut off at a sharp gesture from Raedrick. Their eyes locked and Raedrick could see the defiance, the simmering frustration, even anger, within his friend. He drew in a slow breath and let it out before replying. "It makes sense, Julian. Povol can't paddle, and Ravi will need your help to steer the boat downstream. You don't need me to get Povol to help, but if I can get to this cache before they do -"

"You'll what? Destroy it? Carry it back to town yourself and hope they don't catch up to you and cut you to ribbons? What *exactly* is your plan, Rae?"

Put that way, he was forced to admit it did not sound like the most rational scheme ever. But it had to be done. "I'll get anything valuable and use the other canoe. I can make better distance on the river than they can ashore, and it will remove any reason for them to remain here, or for others to follow in their footsteps."

Julian threw his hands up in frustration.

Raedrick continued on in a rush before he could get a word in edgewise. He leaned forward, speaking in his best command tone. "I'm doing this, Julian. And you're getting Povol back to town for treatment." He paused, then added, "That's an order."

Incredulous did not begin to describe the expression that came over Julian's face. He snorted. "Bollocks. You're not my Squad Leader anymore, Rae. We're *partners*, remember?"

"Then do this in the name of our partnership. If we wait to come back, Geoff and his men may have already retrieved it - "

"Let them. Who cares?"

Raedrick sighed and looked away. "It's not theirs."

Another snort. "No? Then whose is it?"

"They conned it out of Tolburt."

A long second passed before Julian responded. When he did, it was quietly, barely more than a whisper. "Are you...?" He stopped, cleared his throat and looked around as though unable to believe he was actually someplace real. "Are you nuts?" he said in a more normal tone. "What is it with you and him? He sold us out, would have seen us on the gallows to save his own skin, and you act as though you owe him something." Julian spat on the ice. "That's what you owe him Rae, right there. So he got conned. Serves him right. And you..." He shook his head. "You don't need to go getting yourself killed over his sorry ass."

Julian was right, of course. In a fashion. Tolburt had betrayed them, but only after Raedrick had led him into a far greater treason first. Could he really blame the man for trying to do right by himself, in those circumstances?

Yes, a part of Raedrick's mind replied.

He forced that voice down, and with it a flash of bitterness that he thought he had put long behind him. No matter if he had or not. Tolburt had been one of his men - still was one of his. And he had left the man behind, to his fate.

Not this time.

Raedrick reached out and clasped Julian's shoulder, giving it a gentle squeeze. He looked his friend in the eye for a long moment. "I need to do this, Julian."

Julian returned the gaze in silence for a small eternity. Frustration and incredulity battled in his expression until finally they gave way before acceptance. He was not going to talk Raedrick out of this, and he knew it.

Julian nodded and laid his hand atop Raedrick's. He returned the squeeze and cleared his throat. "Povol, Ravi, get in the boat. We're casting off."

The two men exchanged doubtful, confused looks, but complied in silence. No doubt Povol was eager to be off, and the elder Guildsman knew better than to rekindle the argument. The wisdom of age.

Raedrick released Julian's shoulder and took a step back. He nodded once and tightened the straps of his pack. Then, adjusting the fit of his sword belt, he turned and made his way back to the riverbank. Behind him, he heard the soft scrape of ice against the canoe's hull as his friends cast off into the Northflow's current.

He hoped he would see them again.

23

UNDER A ROCK

Raedrick pushed hard, keeping to the river's edge as best he could, to keep his bearings. But Julian had been right: there was no time to lose. Geoff and his remaining men were certainly heading this way, their minds fixed on revenge, and Raedrick had no illusions about his ability to take them on and live.

Maybe if he had his own sword...

No. He still was not proficient with the Tyrashi blade. At least not to the standards he expected of himself. More than once he had considered just giving up on it and returning to his trusty saber. He knew that weapon inside and out, and he knew it was no boast to claim he was a master with it.

His new sword, a gift from his late comrade-in-arms Selam, was another matter entirely. The weight and balance were different, the grip different, the curve of the blade, and the sharpened edge on the back-edge. Even one of those elements would have meant weeks of training to adjust properly. But all of them together... It was a monumental change, requiring different stances and movements than he was used to. And he had no one to teach them to him; the only pattern he had to follow was the memory of how Selam had moved in battle, and he had only fought beside the man for a short time.

It was hopeless. But he could not dishonor Selam by setting his family's sword aside; he had passed it to Raedrick because he lacked a son and his family was dying with him. How could Raedrick refuse a request like that?

And so he had to live up to the man's wishes, learn to wield it in a manner worthy of the honor Selam had displayed, and that he had payed to Raedrick on his death bed.

Not that that would be helpful at all under the current circumstances.

Bloody fool. That bull-headedness of yours is going to get you killed one of these days.

Raedrick chuckled at the little voice in the back of his head. It was probably more right than it knew.

The riverbank twisted and turned as it cut through the mountains to the north, and Raedrick found himself almost reversing course several times. That and the steady uphill grade, shallow as it was, made for slow going even as he pushed himself to greater speed.

At least the snow cover was less along the bank. The terrain was more often bare rock, or covered in ice, and what snow there was had become packed over the weeks of winter, so his trail was less obvious than it would have been in the loose powder deeper in the woods. Small comfort, that.

The sun was a third of the way to its zenith when Raedrick paused and pulled Tolburt's map out again. He studied it for a time, frowning as he pondered. The Northflow was plain on the paper, winding its way past mountains on either side until a small dotted line broke away, toward a strange symbol on the third mountain on the west side: an X within a circle.

X marks the spot.

The problem was, where exactly was it? Raedrick looked

around to get his bearings again. To the east, across the river, lay the northern flank of the mountain he had been trudging past all morning. To the north, more hills and mountains were visible ahead, but just as to the south he could not see far along the river itself before a bend cut off his view.

To the west, though...

The woods along the river obstructed much of his view; he could have marched well past his aim point by now, and not realized it. Povol had said the marking on the map was just a few miles upstream. If he had passed it by, he would be forced to double back, and that could be beyond hazardous with Geoff and company on his trail.

He needed to get to higher ground, take a look around.

Raedrick stuffed the map back into his pocket and made for a nearby tree. Tall and sturdy, it had a few low-hanging limbs that should offer good purchase for climbing.

Ten minutes later, he wedged himself into a nook between a limb that was probably a bit too narrow and the trunk, which was also a bit more spindly at this height - about thirty feet - than he would have preferred. But it held, and he had a commanding view of the area; only a few other trees nearby were as tall as the one he had picked.

From his vantage point, Raedrick could clearly see the slope of the mountain he had been walking past. Though from this distance the peak seemed to scrape the top of the sky, it was quite a bit smaller than the others nearby; Tollard's Peak dwarfed it easily. On this side, the peak was almost completely wooded, the tree line only cutting off on the mountain's top third. In places, the trees were broken by cliff faces and the occasional pile of debris from some ancient rock slide. But that was nothing unusual, and he could see nothing special that would point him one way or another, nothing that hinted at the map's hidden secret.

Wouldn't be much of a secret if it was just lying around, easy to spot.

True enough, but it still irked him. Time was running short; he needed to find this cache, whatever it was, and get out of here. Fast.

But where?

Raedrick took the map out and unfolded it. He spent a long while looking at it, trying to see something - anything - in its simple lines that might help. But there was just the dotted line running from along the river bank, up the flank of the mountain, then around a bend to the circle and X...

He blinked, then looked up at the mountain again.

A bend in the side of the peak. It had to be something prominent, something recognizable...

There. A bit less than a mile further north and a third of the way up the slope - a rocky protuberance that thrust out from the trees. It looked as though maybe it curled back on itself. Maybe there was a little canyon on the other side?

That had to be it; there was nothing else Raedrick saw that could even be close.

Unless you already passed it.

He forced the doubting voice down and re-pocketed the map. Then - slowly, carefully - he made his way down from the tree.

When his feet were back on solid ground, he took a minute to gather himself. Then, trying not to feel the surge of excitement that threatened to well up, he turned away from the river, toward that wall of rock, and set out.

He probably got turned around a half dozen times before he finally stepped out from under the forest's canopy and into the clearing at the base of the protuberance. It could not have been more than a mile from his tree, but it had taken nearly three hours, best he could tell, to get there. It was upslope, sure, but still it should not have taken that long.

Raedrick cursed his lack of bearings, feeling more than a bit disgusted with himself. But then, he should not have been surprised. Orienteering had never been his strong suit, and he did not even have a compass with him for this venture.

Which was stupid in and of itself.

"No sense getting worked up over it," he said aloud to himself.

That only helped a little.

He took a moment and just stood there, breathing deeply to lower his heart rate after the strenuous climb and looking up at the rock face. It certainly was impressive. Craggy, offering many good hand and footholds for someone who had the notion of climbing it, the protuberance thrust up over a hundred feet above him. High up, he thought he could see clumps of branches and twigs in some of the crags - bird nests of some sort, he thought. Here and there, a hardy tree or bush had managed to take root on the side of the cliff as well.

Turning around, he could see the river flowing below, in the valley between the mountains. Further south, the gorge leading down to the lake was more clearly visible.

In all, it was quite a beautiful view. Too bad he did not have time to bask in it.

He followed the rock wall, moving to his right and stepping carefully around the boulders and smaller rocks that littered its base, not a particularly easy task considering many of them were buried in snow and he only learned of their presence when his foot came down and did not go as far into the snow as he expected. After a few steps, he gave up and retreated back to the tree line. At least at the edge of the canopy he could be reasonably sure to avoid the worst of the trip hazards.

The wall continued on, gradually curving away from him so it veered more north than east. And then, all at once, he reached the end. As though someone had sliced the rock with an axe and heaved the excess aside, the wall simply stopped, leaving just the not-so-gently rising slope of the mountain to rise past it.

This had to be the place.

Raedrick gingerly left the trees and made for the end of the rock wall, feeling his way carefully with each step. But for whatever reason, here there were not as many rocks to snag his feet, and within a minute he found himself standing beneath the cliff.

Now what?

The cloven edge of the cliff extended back a good ways, but then seemed to end as it met the mountain's slope. As far as Raedrick could tell, there was nothing else to it.

He frowned. He had been so sure this was the place. There was nothing else that even resembled the drawing on the map. Maybe...

Raedrick flashed back to the cave Povol had led them to during their first night on the mountain. That had been nearly impossible to see. Unless you knew it was there, you could easily walk right past it. If this was similar... He slid his hand along the cliff face and slowly walked back toward where it met with the slope, looking closely at the ground and the cliff itself as he went.

Finally, he saw it. About thirty feet back, concealed by a small bush that grew near the base of the cliff and by the fold of the cliff itself: a small hole, maybe three and a half feet wide and as many tall, leading back into the cliff face.

Raedrick crouched down and peered into the hole, but the early afternoon sun did little to illuminate the interior. After only a couple feet there was nothing to see but shadows and blackness.

Well, what did you expect?

Raedrick snorted and shrugged his pack off, then went back to the tree line. A few minutes later, he came back with a stout branch. He opened his pack and pulled out a scrap of cloth - the remnants of his old shirt - and wound it around the branch. Then he set to with flint and steel.

It took longer than he would have thought, but eventually he got the makeshift torch burning. Replacing the flint and steel into its pouch, he pulled his pack back on then, hefting the torch, he got down on his knees and looked into the little cave mouth again.

Still nothing. The torch would not illuminate anything from out here.

Raedrick took a deep breath, then crouched over and, moving carefully to avoid burning himself in the face, half-crawled into the cave.

24

HIDDEN GEMS

The cave widened slowly as it burrowed into the cliff face until, after about twenty feet, it stretched a good six feet across and five high. Raedrick could walk normally, albeit with a stoop, but that was a far sight better than it had been at the opening.

The walls and ceiling were rough, jagged, but the floor was smooth, as though many feet had tromped through here over the years and wore it down. Or perhaps paws more than feet.

That was a distinct possibility, now that he thought about it. Bears and other animals sought shelter for the winter in caves. Raedrick imagined they would not be pleased to have their slumber disturbed by the likes of him.

He paused mid-step and almost turned around to leave, the thought of an enraged bear tearing him limb from limb giving him pause. But there was no sound, aside from the soft crackle of burning cloth and wood from his simple torch, and the only odors he could detect were woodsmoke - again from the torch - and his own grime from the last several days in the wild. Surely if a creature had made this cave a layer, there would be some sign.

Raedrick drew a deep breath and continued forward.

The passage bent to the right ahead. Raedrick followed and,

after two paces, stopped dead in his tracks again. But this time from amazed surprise more than nervousness.

No sooner had the passage completed its bend than the cave opened wide on all sides, becoming a semi-circular chamber probably thirty feet across and twenty tall at its center. All over the chamber, stalactites hung down from the ceiling, nearly meeting stalagmites, lesser in number, that rose to greet them from the floor. But that was not what amazed him.

There was light here, above and beyond the flickering of his torch. It streamed down from a crack in the ceiling and cast a soft glow over the entire chamber, but particularly on a still pool that sat in the center of the floor. The light struck the water and reflected all around the chamber in glistening waves that seemed to shimmer and move of their own accord.

Strange that, considering the water itself was perfectly smooth.

"Gods be good," Raedrick found himself murmuring. The silent beauty of the place - and it was silent still, except for the noises Raedrick brought with him - seemed to warrant it.

This had to be the place, but he could see no sign of any cache. No structures or furniture. No chests or bags. Nothing to suggest that men had ever set foot here.

It had to be here. But where?

Raedrick frowned and made a slow circle of the chamber, being careful to avoid the pool. The last thing he needed was to get wet, as cold as it was. Although now that he thought of it, it was not nearly as cold here in the cave as it had been outside. That did not change the fact that he would have to head back out, and soon. Getting wet could be a fatal mistake.

But as he completed his circuit, he still could see no sign of the promised cache.

"Damn it," he muttered.

This must be the wrong place. He must have passed the spot. He pulled the map out and unfolded it, then spread it out on the floor and crouched down, holding his torch to fully illuminate it. What had he missed?

Nothing.

He could see nothing in that map to indicate anything he had overlooked outside. The rock face that held this cave was the only formation that fit the drawing on the map. Or at least, the only one he had come across so far. It was possible he had not passed the place up, but had instead stopped to early.

"No, no," he said to himself. That could not be it. This place was too perfect: a well-concealed cave in the cliff face. How many other places like this could there be?

At least one, he thought, recalling Povol's cave again.

Raedrick snorted and pushed himself to his feet, crumpling the map in his hand in frustration as he stood. He did not relish the notion of tromping even further north through the snow and ice, especially with Geoff and his men very likely drawing nearer by the second. But there was no other choice. If this was not the place, then he must…

He stopped, midway through turning back toward the cave entrance. Something glinted at the edge of his vision. What was that?

Slowly, deliberately, he turned to his left, carefully sweeping his gaze over every inch of floor, wall, and ceiling in his field of view, trying once again to see the…

There it was.

Son of a bitch.

It was so obvious, and he had overlooked it completely.

There, in the center of the chamber where the stream of light hit the water from the crack above, something metallic glinted from the bottom of the pool. He moved slightly forward, and the glinting ceased. Slightly back, and it started up again.

Now that was clever. Whatever it was down there had been placed so it would only give itself away if someone was looking for it at exactly the right angle. Lucky that Raedrick had done the circuit, otherwise he would have missed it.

He snorted. He very nearly had missed it anyway.

His heartbeat quickening with sudden excitement, Raedrick

moved to the edge of the pool and squatted down with narrowed eyes. Now that he knew where to look, he could see it plain as day: a small wooden chest, fully submerged in the water - it was hard to tell how far down it was - with brass or gold fittings holding it together. Probably gold, considering it had not tarnished.

A grin spread over Raedrick's face. "Gotcha," he said.

He had found it alright. But how to get to it?

The pool was a good ten feet across, and the chest lay at its exact center. Worse, it lay completely underwater, and the more he looked at it the more certain Raedrick became that it was deeper than arms-reach.

His initial elation - hell, exhilaration - over the find faded as he considered the logistics of it. There was no way he was going to get that thing out of the pool, not without getting soaking wet. And that was not really an option, not if he wanted to keep on living; he did not have time to spend drying off before heading back out into winter's cold.

"Son of a bitch," he said softly.

Now what?

He pondered for a long several moments, but could not think of any way to retrieve the chest short of hopping in the pool. He shook his head. It looked like Julian was right. He might as well leave it and head back; he was never going to hear the end of this one.

The silence of the chamber was broken. A scuff of boots against rock from behind, followed by a shuffling sound caused Raedrick to stiffen.

"Well. Isn't this a cozy place," a voice said from behind him.

❧ 25 ❧

MEET-UP

Raedrick spun as quickly as he could, dropping his torch to the ground and withdrawing the longsword from his belt in one smooth draw as he rose to his full height. In that half-second he forced himself to calm and focused. He could not win, not alone. But he could go down fighting.

His brain fully registered the voice that had spoken at the same instant he completed the turn, and he brought his sword down. He felt the embarrassed scowl growing on his face before he could stop it.

Julian grinned back at him, amused.

"Hi, Rae," he said, eyes flicking up and down over Raedrick's form. "A little jumpy, aren't you?"

Raedrick let out his breath in a rush, letting the last of his tension flow from his body with it. He let his shoulders sag as he grounded the point of his sword, but could not stop the sudden shaking of his limbs from the surge of adrenalin.

Chagrin over being caught by surprise - and being so slow to recognize his friend's voice - chased relief through his psyche. He eyed Julian askance. "What the hell are you doing here?"

Julian shrugged and stepped fully into the chamber, throwing his cloak back over his shoulders as he moved. He carried a torch in his left hand, makeshift like Raedrick's, and wore an unconcerned expression. "Turns out Ravi is quite a lot better with a canoe than he let on. After a few minutes I realized you would probably need my help more than he did, so I had them put me ashore." He looked around the chamber, pursing his lips for a moment, then grinned at Raedrick. "You didn't *really* think I was going to let you do this alone, did you?"

All manner of protests leapt to Raedrick's mind. Reasons beyond number why Julian should not have done that. But right then none of them mattered worth a damn; the gratitude he suddenly felt toward his friend overwhelmed them all.

He opened his mouth to speak, but Julian beat him to it. "This is the place, huh?"

Raedrick cleared his throat and nodded, tucking his sword back behind his belt. "In the pool."

Julian raised an eyebrow and walked over to stand next to him, squinting as he peered into the pool. After a moment, he nodded. "Clever. Sort of. Hope whatever's in that chest holds up well in water."

Raedrick grunted. "The more immediate problem is how to get it out of there."

Julian looked askance at him and almost appeared about to laugh. But then he peered at the pool again and his lips turned downward into a frown. "If we had time, we could build a fire to dry off afterward. But..."

"We don't have the time," Raedrick finished.

Julian nodded emphatically. "We really don't. I'm pretty sure I saw Geoff's men up on the mountain, a few miles back. They're still a ways off, but heading downslope." He left the rest unsaid.

Raedrick bit back a curse. It had only been a matter of time before the ruffians caught up to them; their trail would not be difficult to follow in the snow. It would have been nice if they had a bit more time, though. "Any ideas?"

Julian looked around again, still frowning. "Short of getting a few branches and trying to fish it out...?" He shook his head. "Of course, they can only come at us one at a time through there." He gestured toward the cave entrance. "We could hold this place against them for a year."

Raedrick considered Julian's words for a moment. He did have a point. They could get the chest out and take all the time they needed drying off, and all Geoff could do about it was block them from leaving. It was not like he could come in and take it from both of them, the way the cave was configured.

But then, he did not have to, did he? Merely preventing their escape would be enough. It would not be a protracted siege. Raedrick shook his head. "If we had food we could. For a short while."

"Well then," Julian said, nodding concurrence. "Let's go get some branches."

A quarter of an hour later, near as Raedrick could figure it, they made their way back down the entrance tunnel and into the cave's main chamber, several branches, ranging in length from four to six or seven feet in length, carried between them.

Once inside, they took a moment to examine the pool again, then they both hefted sticks and walked to the water's edge.

The plan was simple enough: push the chest out of the center of the pool with the longest branches, then keep on poking and prodding it until they could get it within arm's reach of the edge. By then, it would be mostly out of the water, and the two of them would just snatch it up.

Raedrick was not entirely sure the notion would work. The pool's bottom looked smooth enough, but in the dim light it was hard to tell for sure, and there could be holes that the chest could catch on. But he did not have a better idea.

Julian hefted his branch and flashed one of his nigh-eternal grins. "All set?"

Raedrick nodded. "Let's see how this does."

He pushed his branch into the pool...

And it skittered atop the surface of the water, not even penetrating an inch.

Shocked, Raedrick dropped the branch, and it clattered to the ground, two thirds of it resting atop the surface of the pool as though it were made of rock.

"What the...?" Julian began, then stopped, his mouth hanging open in astonishment.

Raedrick merely shook his head, at a loss for words.

Julian pressed his own branch into the pool, with the same effect. He raised his hands helplessly and looked at Raedrick in confusion. "How does that work?"

"It must be an enchantment of some kind," Raedrick said, his mind awhirl. It had to be a magical effect, but it was like nothing he had ever seen or heard of. Not that he was an expert on the subject by any means, but he had seen enough to have at least a passing familiarity with what a mage could do.

"Great," Julian muttered. "Where's Melanie when we need her?"

Raedrick shared the sentiment. The presence of Lydelton's mage in residence certainly would be helpful right then. But that was not going to happen. Raedrick scratched at his chin, then crouched down at the edge of the pool and reached down to the water.

"Whoa, Rae," Julian said, the sharpness of his tone bringing Raedrick up short. "If that pool's got spells on it, I'm pretty sure you don't want to be reaching your hand in there."

Raedrick paused, considering Julian's words. He had a good point. Mages could be tricky; there was an excellent chance whoever had laid these enchantments had also spun a number of other magical traps. He had seen their like before. If he were lucky, it would only burn his hand. If he were unlucky... The possibilities for mischief and harm were almost literally endless.

All the same, they needed to find out just how far the enchantment went.

Slowly, he stretched his hand back out toward the water. Next to him, Julian breathed a curse under his breath and took a half-step away. Just in case.

Raedrick's fingers touched the water...

...and slid in effortlessly. The water was beyond frigid; it was the essence of cold itself, unquenchably greedy for any and all warmth. He could feel the heat from his body siphoning out through his fingertips and into the water. Intuitively, he got the sense that the depth of cold within the pool could never be changed; even if it took all of his and Julian's body heat, it would not have warmed up even a hair. The chill began to spread up his arm, and for a moment he almost felt paralyzed.

Then he came back to himself and he jerked his hand away, out of the water. Cursing mightily, he shook the residual water off. Except no water flew from his hand. Not a single drop.

Raedrick blinked, confused, and raised his fingers to eye level. His hand was completely dry, not even a hint that it had just been submerged. Aside from a greenish-blue color in the tips of his fingers, he could not have told anything had just happened.

That color, and the frigid chill that lingered even still.

"Well that didn't work," Julian said, from behind him.

Raedrick cleared his throat. "Almost."

Julian snorted. "You didn't get any farther than that branch did."

It took a minute for Julian's words to sink in. When they did, Raedrick whirled back to him so quickly Julian took a half-step back in surprise. "What are you talking about? I got in the water just fine. It was just," he shuddered slightly, "so cold."

Julian's eyebrows rose, and he stared at Raedrick in silence for a moment.

"What, you didn't see it?"

"Rae, your fingers splayed out like you had just hit a brick wall and you all but bounced off."

Well, that was odd. Raedrick shook his head. "Strange. I could have sworn..." He peered back at the pool, its surface still completely smooth, undisturbed. "It was like the pool was sucking the warmth out of me through my hand. If I had stayed there for just a few moments more, it would have drained me of heat completely."

Another long moment of silence followed, then both of Julian's eyebrows shot upwards again. "It took your body heat." He sounded excited.

Raedrick nodded.

"But it did not wet you at all."

Another nod.

Julian grinned. "I've got it." He turned around and bounded a few steps away to where their lone remaining torch lay smoldering where he had left it, leaning against the cave wall. He hefted it and loosely wrapped another scrap of cloth around the smoldering torch head, then carefully blew onto the torch head in long, slow breaths. After a minute or so, the flame kindled back to life, and Julian grinned at Raedrick. "Let's see what this does."

Raedrick was about to ask him what he thought he was doing, but before he could say a word Julian had crossed the distance to the pool and thrust the burning torch head into it.

As with the dried sticks, the torch did not penetrate the pool at all, and Raedrick almost snorted out a laugh. But then the flame flickered and faded, and a second later extinguished completely. The torch head stopped releasing smoke and, when Julian had withdrawn it, little flecks of frost glistened atop it in the dim light of the cave.

"By the Gods," Raedrick breathed, and Julian nodded in agreement, but his eyes remained fixed on the pool.

"Is it just me, or is it a little bit shallower?"

Raedrick turned his gaze away from the extinguished torch and beheld the pool. At first, it looked exactly the same as it had before Julian hit it with the torch. But then, looking at it more closely...

Feeling his eyes widen, Raedrick nodded, sudden excitement rushing through him. "It is! Hot damn, Julian."

He reached over and clapped his friend on the shoulder. Julian just grinned in satisfaction.

Raedrick was not sure how much time passed. It could not have been long, but time has a way of running past a man when he's busy. And he and Julian were busy indeed, for the next little while, breaking up the branches they had gathered, stacking them into a small pile next to the edge of the pool, and then working the flint and steel on the last of their cloth to get the fire going.

Then they sat back to wait until the branches had well and truly caught.

"Now *that's* nice," Julian said, holding his hands out before the little blaze and grinning again. "All we need now is some sausage and brandy and we could have ourselves a merry afternoon."

Raedrick chuckled, shaking his head. He could not deny the appeal of that idea. If only they had time.

And sausage to roast.

Instead, Raedrick grabbed out a branch that had well and truly caught ablaze - there was not much to hold on to - and cast it onto the pool.

As before, the flame flickered and quickly died, but it took a bit longer than it had with Julian's torch. And this time, the pool was definitely more shallow. It was working.

"How about we just push the whole thing over onto it?"

Raedrick blinked, then nodded. He should have thought of that.

That just left how to go about doing it. Eventually, they just pulled out their swords and pushed at the campfire the same way they had thought to push the chest free of the pool using the branches. It was far from elegant, and the fire lost its carefully constructed geometry, but it worked. Mostly.

At once, Raedrick saw the utility of doing it that way. The fire flickered and faded, but continued to burn, the self-sustaining nature of the burn seeming to resist the heat drain from the pool. Or maybe as the pool was reduced, it lost some of its appetite for heat. Regardless of why, the fire did not go out all at once, but slowly began to dim and fade.

Excitement surged through Raedrick again. He could see the pool shrinking by the second, more rapidly now. The top of the chest was almost clear.

"More wood!" he said, automatically reverting to a tone of command. "Quickly!"

Julian, to his credit, did not question or hesitate. He could see what was happening just as well as Raedrick. At once, he turned and hurried out of the cave entrance.

He was not gone long, though it seemed to take forever as Raedrick watched the fire gradually die despite all his efforts to sustain it: blowing on it, feeding it what few burnable objects he could find, and hoping. When Julian finally returned with a moderately-sized bundle of branches tucked under his arm, there was not much left burning in the formerly bright and cheerful blaze.

"Hurry," Raedrick urged, not taking his eyes from the dying fire. "We're almost out of time."

Julian dropped the branches with a clatter and began breaking them into smaller pieces. "Seems like I always pull your chestnuts out of the fire," he said with a smirk as brought the first stack over to Raedrick.

Raedrick could not help chuckling. Carefully setting the new wood atop the dwindling fire, he sat back on his heels impatiently. The wood was cold, partially frozen and likely entrained with water. It would take a while to catch. If the pool drained the last of the fire's heat before it could light the new wood…

He need not have worried. Before long, the new wood caught. He and Julian fed larger and thicker pieces of wood and soon enough the fire was blazing merrily again. He looked to the side, judging how long the new stack of wood would last.

"We're probably going to need more. How much light do we have left outside?"

Julian shrugged. "Maybe an hour." He met Raedrick's gaze for a moment, then he sighed. "Alright, alright." He turned toward the entrance again, with a dejected slump to his shoulders that Raedrick just knew was fake. "I'll be back in a bit."

He slipped out, leaving Raedrick alone with the fire once more. There he sat, his back to the entrance, and watched, periodically adding another piece of wood to the fire as it faded. But his eyes never left the steadily lowering fluid of the pool, and the treasure sitting in its center.

❧ 26 ❧

FOOLS GOLD

By the time Julian returned again, the remaining wood was nearly gone, but virtually nothing remained of the pool.

Raedrick had had to shove the fire further down into the pit twice, each time fearing he would douse the flames by moving it too quickly and scattering the fuel. But each time it remained lit, as much as it could while in contact with the heat-draining enchantment.

"Almost there," Julian said, sounding relieved, as he dropped the fresh wood next to Raedrick and began breaking it up.

Raedrick nodded, grabbing up a piece and snapping it in two before dropping it onto the fire. "Shouldn't be long now." He frowned, gauging the pool's remaining depth. "We could probably reach the chest and haul it out now, actually." There was one rock in particular that now protruded from the surface of the pool. If one of them got onto that, he could reach the chest easily enough.

Julian looked sidelong at him, then shook his head. "If it's all the same to you I'd rather not. No telling what else that stuff will do." He·pointed toward the pool's remaining fluid with a stick.

Raedrick considered for a moment. He had a point. You never

knew what an enchantment might do, and their process was working. No sense rushing if they had the time. But did they?

"Did you see any sign of Geoff and his men?"

Julian shook his head, but frowned. "The sun'll be below the mountains soon, though. Can't imagine they're that far behind."

"We may have to risk it."

Raedrick stood and walked slowly around the pool to the closest point to that rock near the chest. About three feet away from where he stood now, and maybe a foot from the chest itself, it was rounded, but large enough to stand on easily, and looked to be completely dry. Strange that. Or maybe not. Memory of how the fluid felt came rushing back: cold, endless cold, but not wet. Not at all.

"I really don't think this is a good idea, Rae. It'll only be a few more minutes with the fire."

Raedrick nodded. "Just don't say I told you so if this doesn't work." Then he hopped over onto the exposed rock.

Naturally, his right foot slipped on the rounded surface of the rock and he lost his balance. For a second, he flailed about, trying to reclaim his balance, then seemingly slowly, he fell forward.

Julian cried out, "Rae!" and rushed forward, but he could not get close enough to help, not in time.

Raedrick was going over. He was going to fall into that bottomless well of cold, and it would devour him. There would be no pulling himself out if his entire body fell in, he was sure of that. He flung out his hands, seeking something, anything, to cling on to.

And they came down on the chest.

Abruptly, his fall stopped. He stood balanced on his left foot, with his hands atop the chest, but he was no longer falling.

He let his breath out in a rush, relief flooding through him. Then a chill deeper than the deepest winter night ran up his right leg. He looked down in chagrin to see his boot partially submerged in the pool. The heat rushed from his body, through his leg, and he felt himself growing weaker. He began to shiver and...his breath frosted in front of his face, despite the warmth of the cave.

Oh Gods, he had caught himself, but not in time. The cold. It was eating him alive. Consuming him.

He had almost no strength left, but maybe he could...

Raedrick pulled upward on his leg with all his might. For a second, he could not move it. Then, all at once, as though he had been pulling on a tense rope that parted, his foot sprang free of the fluid.

He almost overbalanced again, but he managed to bring the boot down atop the rock. It was glossy - covered in a film of ice, and Raedrick found he could not move his toes.

"Son of a bitch," he groaned, but it was weak; he could barely hear his own words.

"Rae, are you ok?"

He just perched there for a moment, shivering uncontrollably and not daring to move. Then he managed to croak out, "Yeah" in a loud enough tone to carry. He drew in a deep breath. "Fire," he said, and then his voice failed him.

Julian nodded, then hurried away, out of Raedrick's line of sight. He heard his friend bustling around busily for several moments that felt like an eternity. Then, slowly, he came back into view. Under his left arm he carried a small bundle of wood. In his right hand he carried a burning stick; he must have fished it out of the fire.

"Hold on, Rae," he said, and he set the burning stick down at the edge of the pool nearest Raedrick, then carefully piled the other wood atop it. An eternity later, another little fire burned there, sending heat Raedrick's way.

It burned like the sun, it was so hot. But he knew that was only in comparison with the infinite cold he had just felt. Slowly, ever so slowly, his shivering slowed and he felt strength returning to his limbs. He managed to raise his ice-logged boot to hold it closer to the fire. It hurt, Gods did it hurt, but it was good also. He imagined he could actually feel the blood thawing in his foot, the capillaries expanding, and circulation returning.

He set his foot down on the rock again and drew a deep breath, then let it out and tried to tell himself he did it without a sob.

Julian crossed his arms over his chest. "I told you - "

Raedrick shot a glare at him, and he stopped. He merely shook his head with a wry expression on his face that did not extend to his eyes, which were still deeply concerned. Raedrick sighed. "I'll be alright," he said, more forcefully. "That fire works wonders."

"How about you let it work back over here, away from that… whatever it is." Julian waved his hand at the remaining fluid in the pool. There was now maybe an inch of the stuff left, but after his last experience Raedrick did not fool himself that it was anything less than deadly.

He pushed off the chest and forced his weight fully back onto his feet. His right foot was still mostly numb, the parts that were not were a mass of pins and needles, so he nearly lost his balance again. He forced himself to stay in place. "We don't have…"

"Rae, get back here. I'll get the damn thing out, ok?" From the tone of Julian's voice, he was about ready to jump the distance himself, throw Raedrick over his shoulder, and haul him back. And to blazes if there was enough room for that.

Raedrick sighed and nodded, turning away from the chest. He winced as he bent his knees to make the short leap across the pool. But when he got there and sat down next to the fire, he had to admit Julian was right - it was far better there, and the fire warmed him far more quickly.

Julian sat down next to him. He said nothing; just watched the pool as its liquid level continued to lower steadily. Across the way, where their first fire had been, a veritable bonfire was burning; Julian must have tossed all the remaining wood onto it before coming to help Raedrick. No wonder the liquid level was dropping as quickly as it was. For that matter, the fire was not fading as quickly, either. The enchantment must have almost run its course.

Julian noticed his gaze and smirked at him. "That's right. We're waiting until the fire does the job on the pool for us. I'm not as dumb as you are."

Raedrick felt himself scowling before he could stop himself. Julian was right. This time. He thought about protesting anyway, but the fire's restorative heat felt too good. Instead, he said, "We need to hurry."

Julian looked at him as though he were daft, but nodded. "Sun's almost down and they'll have a hard time following our trail after dark dark. Moon won't rise for a long time still." He stood and brushed his hands off on the thighs of his leggings. "Now that I think about it, we're probably ok. If they haven't found us yet - "

He broke off talking as a metallic clank issued from the entrance passage, followed by a soft curse.

"Ah hell," Julian muttered.

Raedrick was forced to agree.

27

THE DREAMS OF AVARICE

Raedrick tried to push himself to his feet, but found his right leg would still not support his weight very well and he stumbled back to the ground. He gritted his teeth to try again; he needed to be up and ready for action if that was one of Geoff's men coming through the passage - and who else could it be?

But Julian beat him to it, bounding past the little fire and actually giving him a little shove back to the ground. "Stay there," Julian ordered, skirting around one of the few stalagmites on this side of the pool and pressing his back to the wall of the cave. Then he slid slowly toward the entrance and pulled out his knife.

Raedrick understood at once. The person coming in would have seen the light of their fires reflecting down the passage. He knew someone was there, but not how many. If he rounded the corner and only saw Raedrick…

The light from a torch appeared in the passage and a burly man dressed in furs - dog furs no doubt - rounded the corner. Not just burly - the man was tall. Huge. Raedrick recognized him immediately as one of Geoff's men; his height was distinctive, and his face was crisscrossed with tears and bite wounds - the calling card of one of Povol's dogs. He carried a lit torch in his left hand.

He wore a longsword on his left hip and the straps of a backpack were visible on his shoulders.

Their eyes met across the cavern and the thug grinned, showing more missing teeth than not. Then he turned his head and bellowed, "He's here," back down the passage.

So much for silencing him before he could make a report.

The thug stepped into the cavern, keeping his eyes locked on Raedrick. His free hand drifted down to the pommel of his sword. "Constable, you've got a world of hurt coming your - "

The rest of his words were cut off in a grunt of surprise that became a yelp of pain as Julian moved on him. Striking from behind the big man and to his right, Julian grabbed the bandit by the side of his neck and plunged his knife into the his side.

The yelp became a bellow and the big man went down, hard and without a semblance of grace. His gloating expression faded completely, replaced by a grimace of pain as he rolled over onto his back clutching at his injured side. His eyes, wide with confusion, swept around, finally coming to rest of Julian as he wiped the blood off his knife.

"You bastard!" cried the stricken thug from between clenched teeth.

Julian shook his head and drove his boot into the big man's temple. The bandit's eyes rolled in his head and he fell limp. "My parents were married," Julian said, coldly. Then he wiped his knife off and sheathed it. He looked over at Raedrick, his expression all business. "Can you walk? We need to get moving."

Raedrick shrugged and pushed himself up off the ground. Moving more slowly, he found he was able to gain his feet without overbalancing. Gingerly, he moved his so-recently frozen foot forward and shifted his weight.

A hundred little knives shoved themselves into the foot, and he gasped. But the foot held up and he was able to keep his balance as he finished the step.

Julian frowned. He did not need to say it; they were going to have to move faster than that if they were going to get out of this.

Geoff's band numbered five more. Long odds under good circumstances. Odds they had faced and overcome before, but they were weary, hungry, and he had a sword he was not used to. That just made the odds worse.

Julian ducked into the entrance, keeping his back against the rock wall, and peeked around the corner. Whatever he saw made him cringe back, quickly.

"They're not coming in," he said as he moved quick to Raedrick's side. "Yet. But there's at least one more of them right outside the cave. He shouted for our friend there," he gestured at the unconscious man, "wanted to know what was going on."

"It won't be long, then."

Julian shook his head.

He was right; they needed to go. Raedrick looked aside, at the chest, now all but completely free of the pool's fluid. Less than a quarter of an inch looked to go before the chest would be out. They were so close; it would be a shame to leave without what they came for, to leave it to the scum who conned Tolburt.

Julian groaned softly, shaking his head. Then he walked over to the unconscious thug and, grasping him by the shoulder, rolled him over onto his side. The movement revealed his wound, and Raedrick could see blood still flowing. Slowly; not spurting, but it still flowed. He would be in trouble in a few minutes if the bleeding continued like that. But Julian paid that no mind. He set to work getting the man's pack off.

"Can't lug that chest around very quickly," he muttered as he pulled the man's first arms out of the shoulder strap. Then he pushed the man over so he lay face-down on the ground. "But we don't really need to, do we?" He made short work of the other strap, then he stood and hurried over to the rock Raedrick had nearly fallen off earlier.

The pool was much reduced and Julian had no trouble stepping on to the rock. Then he crouched down and rummaged through the thug's pack for a moment. He pulled a small implement of some kind out and unsheathed his knife, then he leaned forward, obscuring Raedrick's view of the chest.

"What are you doing?"

"Laremy," Julian stopped speaking and muttered a curse softly, then resumed whatever it was he was doing, "showed me how to open up a lock once."

Raedrick blinked, surprise preventing any response. "Ah," was all he could manage after a moment. He had not realized any of his men had such…eclectic…skills.

No time to worry about it now. Laremy was long gone and Julian…Julian was not his subordinate anymore, was he? And besides, they had moments at best before the rest of Geoff's thugs came charging in.

Raedrick picked up his longsword from where he had set it when he went to work on the fire, seemingly so long ago, and stepped over toward the cave entrance. It was getting easier to move; each step brought less pain - more like pins and needles than daggers now - and his balance was less awkward. He stopped next to the fallen thug and listened carefully. Julian was making enough noise with his tinkering, but if anyone was coming into the cave, Raedrick ought to hear it.

Nothing.

It was too much to hope the man outside had left. At best he was waiting for the rest of his companions to reinforce him before he came in after them. At worst… At worst they were all there concocting something dreadful for him and Julian.

Raedrick adjusted his grip on his sword and settled into a ready stance. His left foot slipped on the ground, and he looked down to find the rock at his feet slick with blood from the unconscious man.

That would not do, not at all.

It took Julian longer to get the lock open than he thought it would. Granted, he had not even tried to pick a lock in quite some time; certainly not since he became a law man. Just try explaining that one to the mayor.

He snorted softly at that thought.

His knife caught on something inside the lock and twisted in his hand, and he nearly dropped it into the whatever it was that made up the pool. He was not going to go into *that* stuff after the knife. No way. Gritting his teeth, he adjusted his grip and re-inserted the slender blade, then held it steady as he fished around with the narrow metal file he had found in the thug's pack. He must have been handy with a lock, too, that one.

He heard Raedrick pacing around behind him, and Julian could practically hear it in his friend's footsteps: hurry up!

And he was right. The longer they remained here the more likely they were not going to get out at all.

The knife slipped again and Julian almost gave up right then and there. Whatever was in this chest was not worth their lives. Best they get rolling.

He looked over his shoulder to tell Raedrick as much and saw that he was crouched over the fallen bandit. What was he - ? Oh, he was bandaging the man's wound, where Julian had stabbed him.

Always the softy, Raedrick was.

Julian found himself chuckling, and he shook his head. Then he turned back to the chest, his thought of leaving going unspoken. Just like he would not just let that bandit bleed out, Rae would not go without Tolburt's loot, whatever it was, and to blazes with being smart about it.

Better get this stupid thing open, so we can get out of here.

He set to the lock again, jabbing the knife in a bit harder than he intended to. It caught on something and stuck fast.

Julian frowned. That was probably not good. He probed with the file around where the knife's blade was sunk and felt something he had not noticed before. A little protuberance. He twisted the file counterclockwise, and…

The lock clicked and the lid of the chest shifted, ever so slightly. It was open.

For a second, Julian sat there in surprise. That was…easy. Sort of. Easier, in the end, than a chest like that had a right to be.

But then again, the magical pool was more than lock enough, wasn't it?

Julian yanked the knife out and examined the blade; it was notched in a couple places, but not too badly. Nothing a bit of time with a whetstone would not cure. He slipped it into his belt and put the file away. Then he gripped the chest's lid with both hands and lifted it open.

He looked inside, and found himself frozen in place by shock.

28

BESIEGED

"Um… Rae, you want to take a look at this."

Raedrick pulled the makeshift bandage tight around the thug's belly and looked back at Julian. He sat crouched on the rock island, such as it was, and had the chest open. But his tone said what was inside the chest was not good.

Raedrick pushed himself to his feet, suppressing a grunt as the pins and needles stabbed into his foot again. He hobbled, still more slowly than he would prefer, over to the edge of the nearly-vanished pool.

"What is it?"

Julian rose to his feet and hopped off the rock and back to the edge of the pool. "Tolburt wasn't the only one who got conned." He held out a folded piece of parchment.

Curious, but with a sinking feeling in his gut, Raedrick took the parchment, yellowed with age and torn about the edges, and unfolded it. "What is…"

He stopped speaking as he saw, written in a firm hand, a simple message on the parchment. "You've done well to get this far, Kalem, but this was just the first step. Your birthright awaits you at the Falconer's Stairs, if you prove worthy." There was no signature.

"There is nothing else in the chest," Julian said as Raedrick looked up from the note. He jabbed his finger at the parchment. "Just that."

"You're kidding."

Julian's scowl would have knocked over a bear at ten paces. "Do I look like I'm kidding, Rae?" He threw up his hands and stalked away from the pool. "I *told* you not to get involved in this. Tolburt didn't deserve it, and it was trouble we didn't need. But *no*. You had to go and be all *noble*." He whirled around again, facing Raedrick fully, thrusting his index finger at him like a lance. "All of this, the fighting, nearly getting ourselves killed. And *this* is what we get for it? A bloody riddle?"

His last question ended in a shout that echoed around the cavern for a couple seconds.

Raedrick had no response for a moment. He looked back down at the page, reading it over again. He frowned. "Who's Kalem, I wonder?"

He looked up to see Julian looking at him incredulously. "Who cares?"

"Well there's clearly something to be found. Looks like this was part of a right of passage for this Kalem, and coming here was just the first step. If we can find out who he is…"

Julian cut him off. "We'll do what, go off on some loony quest for," he waved his hands around aimlessly, "whatever his birthright is? *Was*?" He snorted. "Probably a half acre of rocky ground with a couple sheep on it."

Raedrick opened his mouth to reply, but Julian kept right on going.

"Not that we'll get a chance, because Geoff and his boys will probably gut us in a few minutes. How - "

Just then the fire they had lit atop the pool's fluid popped and went out, leaving only the little fire Julian had lit to warm Raedrick after his near miss, and the thug's torch where it lay on the cavern floor. The comparatively dim illumination was like evening compared with midday. Julian snarled a curse and turned away from him, stalking over toward where the torch lay.

He was right, of course. Whoever Kalem was, and whatever this birthright of his might be, it would have to wait. The priority now had to be getting out of there with their skins intact. Raedrick again drew a breath to speak, and was again cut off.

"Everything all right in there, Constable?"

Geoff's voice came from through the entrance passage, and Raedrick stiffened. Julian spun toward the entrance, drawing his sword. They waited for a long moment, but neither Geoff nor his men came into view.

Raedrick moved even with Julian and, stuffing the parchment into his pocket, hefted his sword. He tried to feel confident in his prospects with the unfamiliar blade, but given his lack of mobility...

"Constable?"

Closer to the entrance now, it was obvious to Raedrick that the thug had not come inside; he was shouting from outside the cave.

"He's just trying to spook us," Julian said, softly. "Make us do something stupid."

Raedrick shrugged. "He knows we're in here." He raised his voice. "We're doing great, Geoff, thanks. Your friend says hi. He's taking a nap right now."

"I'm surprised to hear that." His chuckle sounded more than a little disturbing as it echoed down the passage. "So we've got a little problem here. You've got what I want. I could take it, but frankly you've cost me too many men already."

Julian grinned wolfishly. "We can cost you a few more if you'd like," he shouted back.

Speaking of doing something stupid...

"Didn't realize you had someone else with you, Constable." Julian blanched a little. "How about this? You come on out, nice and quiet, and bring me what's mine, and we can all go about our business. Nice and easy, no more trouble."

"Yeah right," Julian muttered. "I believe that as much as one of Horace's sea stories."

Raedrick chuckled. "Horace's fishing stories are more honest." He raised his voice again. "How do I know you'll keep your side of it?"

"You don't," came the reply. "But I can sit out here 'til spring if I have to. We could have a right fun time of it, eh boys?" He paused, no doubt waiting for his men's response, which did not travel as well down the tunnel. "How long can you last in there, Constable?"

And that was the question of the day, wasn't it? Raedrick looked back at the little fire beside the pool and the torch, both already beginning to dwindle as their fuel burned away. Before long he and Julian would be left completely in the dark. And then what?

Julian saw it too. His frown spoke volumes. "There's some food in that guy's pack," he nodded at the still prone thug. "But..." He let the rest go unsaid.

They could not stay here long. The longer they waited, the less tenable their position became. Geoff's offer, dishonest as it likely was, was their only option.

"Give us a minute to talk it over in here," Raedrick shouted.

"Of course," came the reply. It positively dripped with gloating superiority.

❦ 29 ❦

COMING TO TERMS

"Y ou ready?" Raedrick asked Julian, and received a shrug
in return.

"Don't see any point in waiting." Julian tugged at the
strips of cloth he had fashioned into a rope. It would not do for
those knots to let go. "How 'bout you, big fellow?"

The thug who had attacked them in the cave grunted and tried
to say something, but all that came through the gag Julian had
forced into his mouth was a muffled bit of gibberish.

Julian looked back at Raedrick and flashed a nervous grin.
"Let's do it," he said. Then he gave the thug a shove between his
shoulder blades to set him to walking, and followed him into the
tunnel leading outside.

Raedrick paused only to pick up the chest. It was not particularly large, but it was solidly built and heavier than it looked;
good thing he would not have to carry it far. Then he followed.

The thug had begun to come around almost immediately after
their exchange with Geoff, and it was then that Raedrick had
come up with the plan.

Plan. That made it sound like something more than what it really was: a desperate gamble. But it might work.

They had made quick work of tying the still stunned man up and gagging him, then Raedrick went back to the end of the tunnel to banter with Geoff, hoping to delay him long enough for Julian to get the chest out of the pool completely.

It had almost not worked. The chest had proven impossible to lift until Julian had just tossed the last of their fire onto the surface of the fluid. Praise the gods, there had been enough fuel left for the fire to reduce the pool to just below the bottom of the chest, and he had managed to lift it up and out of the depression where it had lain for who knows how long.

And now they were slinking their way through the tunnel out of the cave, Julian and the thug leading the way and Raedrick bringing up the rear. Julian had his knife out in his right hand and the torch in his left, and he kept the thug moving with gentle - or not so gentle - prods with the knife.

"We're coming out," Raedrick yelled. Geoff and his men had certainly seen them coming, but it could not hurt to give a little warning as well. The plan was simple, but delicate. Any number of things could go wrong, almost from the start, but there was no other course open to them.

The real difficulty began when the ceiling had lowered to the point they all had to crouch down. Julian could still urge the prisoner ahead, but for Raedrick, carrying that chest while doubled over... It was a relief when they finally emerged into the open air.

Almost.

Julian and the prisoner got out first, and Julian promptly tossed the torch to the ground and grabbed the big thug by the back of his shoulder, pulling him back against his body and placing the knife against his throat. "No one come any closer," he ordered in his battlefield voice.

Raedrick hurried to follow, and found himself facing a semi-circle of five armed men, Geoff in the center. The men were rather worse for wear. One of them, standing immediately to Geoff's right, had a bandage wrapped tightly around his thigh, where Julian had shot him earlier. The two to the right wore bandages on their arms and lower legs, the other victims of Povol's dogs. Besides Geoff himself, only the bandit to Raedrick's extreme left, a fellow who was little more than skin and bones, bore no injuries, but even he looked haggard; they had passed several unpleasant and wearying days. Good to know he and Julian were not the only ones.

The sky to the east was pink-orange with the last vestiges of sunset; overhead, the first stars were visible. A short way away, under the forest canopy in the direction of the river, a fire was burning and Raedrick could make out the outlines of tents. He had a flashback of their first meeting for a second, except Geoff had no falsely magnanimous look about him this time.

Geoff was just opening his mouth - to retort no doubt - when Raedrick emerged. Geoff's lone good eye widened noticeably when he saw the chest Raedrick carried. All around the semicircle, Geoff's men grinned. The skinny one nudged his neighbor with his elbow and said something softly, causing the other man to chuckle.

Geoff's glare put an end to that. "Thought you'd go looking for it," he said, turning his attention back to Raedrick. He grinned broadly. "Couldn't resist the thought of all that gold, could ya?"

Raedrick did not bother to contradict him. "Here's how this works. I'll leave the chest here. We'll go that way." He nodded toward the south. "Once we're clear, we'll let your friend here go, and everyone leaves happy."

"Very generous of you," Geoff said, mockingly.

Raedrick took a step forward and dropped the chest, then rolled his shoulders to relieve the kinks that had developed while he was bent over. "No good to us anyway," he said. "Damn thing's locked."

The group of bandits laughed at that.

Julian began inching to the right, pulling at the prisoner to keep him close, and Raedrick moved to join him, trying to ignore the pins and needles in his foot and walk normally.

"Yep, that's mighty generous," Geoff said. "Problem is, you killed some of my friends." His grin turned vicious. "Can't let that lie." He nodded. "Boys."

As one, the thugs began to close in.

30

MELEE

There was only a second to respond before the bandits fell on them, but Julian did his part without hesitation. He drove his knife into shoulder muscles on the side of the prisoner's neck and shoved him forward into the path of the closest bandit on the right. The wound would not kill him, but it would bleed like crazy; hopefully seeing their comrade bleeding from a neck wound would make at least one of Geoff's men stop to tend to him.

Raedrick had his sword out and was moving before Julian finished, leaping toward the next bandit on the right.

The man was not expecting him to charge, that much was plain from the look of baffled surprise on the man's face. But he was not unskilled either. He veered to Raedrick's left, getting out of the path of his charge and cutting downward viciously.

Which was just what Raedrick was waiting for.

He shifted his sword into his left hand and dropped his weight onto his rear as he went to the ground, sliding through the snow beneath the bandit's cut. No sooner had the bandit's blade whistled past his ear than Raedrick stabbed upward with his own weapon. The man's eyes widened in shocked surprise that turned to pain as Raedrick's sword punctured his left leg at the hip.

The bandit went down, clutching at the wound and screaming, and Raedrick kicked himself up to his feet.

He very nearly went down again when his right foot caught most of his weight. For a second it was as though his ankle had lost every bit of support structure it had ever had and he was going to go down. Then he got his other foot beneath him and managed to stumble into a mostly balanced stance.

He looked behind himself and saw Julian bounding away from the re-wounded prisoner. The prisoner was firmly entangled with his comrade, who had apparently ran straight into him and taken the two of them down in a tangle of limbs.

The two bandits who had been to their left when they came out of the tunnel were moving forward, but one of them - the skinny one - had eyes only for the chest, and the other was hampered by his wounded leg.

Geoff... Raedrick expected him to be enraged, but the bandit leader looked calm, even amused. His eyes met Raedrick, and Geoff raised his finger to his brow in a little salute. Then he stalked forward toward the chest.

Apparently his lost comrades were not all that important, after all.

No time for wondering about Geoff's motivations. Raedrick turned and followed Julian into the quickly darkening forest.

Of course, it was never going to be as simple as that.

No sooner had he passed the first of the trees than Raedrick heard Geoff's voice rise in a loud cry of anger. He must have opened the chest and seen the nothing that resided within. That did not take long.

Raedrick cursed under his breath and pushed himself to greater speed, but there was only so fast a man could run in ankle-deep snow. If only they could have found a way to lock the cursed chest again...

No time to dwell on that.

"Won't be long now," Julian said from a few paces ahead. He ducked beneath a particularly low tree limb, then came to an abrupt halt. "Ah hell."

Raedrick followed suit, stopping at his friend's side, and immediately mirrored Julian's curse.

In front of them, the terrain fell away a good thirty feet or so in a sheer cliff. He could just make out boulders in the growing dark, clustered around the bottom of the drop-off.

"Won't be going that way," Julian muttered.

Raedrick looked left and right. The cliff face ran as far as he could see, which admittedly was not very far. What was this? He did not recall any cliffs like this when he walked up to the cave before. He looked up and realized the problem immediately: instead of running more or less south, they had bent eastward, going more directly downslope toward the river.

"We'd better head back a ways," Raedrick said, turning his back on the drop-off. "I don't want to stumble back onto this after it gets full dark."

Julian grunted, scowling, but he did not voice an objection. There was none to make.

Raedrick took the lead, pushing past the low tree limb and hurrying upslope about fifty feet. There he turned left and set out to the south again, more slowly this time. The light was all but gone, and the danger of falling into some hidden hazard loomed large. With luck, maybe the thugs would follow their first trail to the drop-off and...

Behind him, Julian cried out, and there was a muffled thump of a body falling to the ground.

Raedrick spun around, bringing his sword to bear, and saw his friend lying face-first on the ground. One of the thugs, the fellow who had tripped over their prisoner Raedrick thought, lay atop Julian where he had tackled him.

Raedrick froze for a second, surprise stealing his initiative as he pondered how the man had gotten to them so quietly.

Of course, he would not have had to be terribly quiet; they were making plenty of noise. And he had probably just been following their trail when they appeared right in front of him, and it would not have taken much to sprint across the intervening distance...

Julian twisted beneath the thug, but the man had the advantage of leverage and he forced Julian back to the ground. "I've got them!" he bellowed, and drew a knife from his belt.

Raedrick snapped himself from his reverie and hurled himself forward toward the thug. The thug had no sword; his knife would be poor defenses against Raedrick's attack, so Raedrick simply thrust straight at the thug's heart.

He should not have been surprised when the thug saw him coming and leaped to the side, avoiding his attack, but he was. The man had not looked all that nimble earlier.

Raedrick took a second to regain his footing. That was all the time the thug needed to regain his as well. The two stared at each other over the span of six or seven feet. The thug wet his lips, and Raedrick could just see the man's eyes flicker from Raedrick's sword to his own small knife, then to the ground to Raedrick's left. Raedrick took a quick glance in that direction and saw a sword - the thug's apparently, where he had dropped it during the tackle.

Idiot.

"Better run," Raedrick said, turning his attention back to the thug.

Off to the side, Julian found his feet again and picked up his own weapon.

The thug looked between the two of them and swallowed.

"Go," Raedrick said, nodding back toward the cave, and the thug's comrades. Hopefully the fellow would choose discretion over valor. Raedrick had no doubt he and Julian could take him, but the other men could not be far behind.

It was as though the thought had summoned them. The shadows to the left moved, and with a loud cry, skin-and-bones bounded forward. The last remnants of the sunset flashed off his blade as he crossed in front of his comrade and sent the cutting edge toward Raedrick's neck.

Raedrick hopped backwards and the sword whistled harmlessly through the air in front of him, then he advanced, his own weapon dipping quickly downward before becoming a rising thrust at the man's solar plexus.

Steel met steel with a loud CLANG as skin-and-bones knocked the thrust aside. His lips twisted into a sneer of contempt, and he shuffled forward, swinging backhanded at Raedrick's face with the pommel of his sword.

Again Raedrick backpedaled, but the thug was coming on too quickly; Raedrick would not get away by retreat alone.

So he dropped to the ground and kicked his feet upward.

The thug's eyes widened as his own momentum drove himself into Raedrick's kick. He half-coughed, half-groaned and stumbled off to Raedrick's right, all thought of the fight gone as he tried to recover the breath that had completely left his lungs.

Raedrick shoved himself to his feet. He glanced at the stumbling, coughing thug and dismissed him as not an immediate threat, then peered around to find the other fellow.

In the deepening gloom, he could only see two shadows grappling at each other, each trying in vain to gain an advantage over the other and force him to the ground. Raedrick was reminded of the wrestling matches his Army unit had engaged in during the long months of relative inactivity before the war had really caught fire. He recalled Julian was pretty good at wrestling.

He was also exhausted and still harboring the wounds of his previous captivity, though he was loathe to admit it. This was not going to end well.

Raedrick hurried toward his friend and the first thug. As he drew nearer he was able to make out more details. Julian with his left hand on the thug's right wrist, working to keep the knife away from himself. His other arm entwined in the thug's where the man had gotten inside Julian's sword swing. He would not last long with his weaker hand against the thug's stronger.

The two wrestling men turned, bringing the thug's back to Raedrick, and he raised his sword.

Suddenly the thug gave a jerk, twisting his torso away from Julian and wrenching Julian's shoulder. Hard. Raedrick heard the pop a split second before Julian cried out in sudden pain. His right hand went limp and his sword dropped to the ground. His left arm seemed to lose all strength, and the thug's knife moved inexorably plunged toward Julian's body.

There was no time to think, so Raedrick did not. He simply thrust.

The resistance when the tip of his sword entered the thug's back was less than Raedrick expected; it must have slipped between two ribs. But the result was immediate. The knife fell from fingers that were suddenly limp and the thug sagged, forcing Raedrick's blade down with the weight of his body as he breathed out a long gurgling breath. Then he fell forward at Julian's feet, slipping off the sword as he went.

Julian staggered backwards, his left hand moving to his throat as though to make sure his flesh was still intact. Then he gave a little shiver and slumped back against a nearby tree. "That was close," he murmured.

Raedrick nodded, pausing to wipe his sword free of blood and shove it back behind his belt. Then he picked up one of the swords lying on the ground and offered Julian his hand. "We need to move."

Julian glanced aside at skin-and-bones, who was had still not begun to recover his bearings. Raedrick could not see it in the gloom, but he was sure Julian raised a questioning eyebrow at him. Raedrick shook his head; no need to harm skin-and-bones further, not if they could help it.

Julian shrugged. Or tried to; the movement instead produced a hiss followed by a groan of pain.

Raedrick helped his friend away from the tree then,

supporting him with one arm wrapped around his good shoulder, the two of them set off south.

"I think," Julian said through clenched teeth, "it's well past time we went home."

Raedrick was forced to agree with him.

31

EVASION

They walked for a time, slowly at first. But after a few steps, Julian regained his equilibrium and he was able to make a better pace. They soon lost sight of the fallen thug and his stunned companion, but not before the latter managed to regain his feet. Raedrick looked back and saw him, a shadow against the lighter shadow of the snow-covered ground, stumble over to where the other man lay. He checked on his companion then stood, looking at Raedrick and Julian. For a moment, Raedrick thought sure he would charge after them. But instead, skin-and-bones turned and hurried away, back toward the cave and their camp.

"He'll be back with his friends," Julian said. He too had stopped to look back.

Raedrick shook his head. "Only five remain, and two are too injured to fight effectively." The fellow who had taken the arrow to his thigh would not make a difficult opponent, and the man they had held prisoner would be in no shape for fighting for a long time. "I think Geoff's band is done for this fight."

Julian gave him a skeptical look, but did not press the subject.

A few minutes later, Raedrick decided they had put enough distance between themselves and the camp that he could afford to take a look at Julian's latest injury. He did not protest that he was fine when Raedrick suggested they stop. That was a bad sign.

He did protest while Raedrick helped him out of his pack, coat, and shirts - all four of them. Quite vociferously, if not particularly loudly; even in the pain of moving his injured limb, Julian remembered the need for as much stealth as they could muster.

It could have been worse. Near as he could tell, Julian's right shoulder was dislocated. Raedrick had feared he had a broken bone; there would be little he could do about that. But he knew a fix for a dislocation. Julian had performed a similar service for him not so long ago. He recalled it hurt like mad, but it worked.

"This is going to hurt," he said as he grasped Julian's arm.

"What doesn't?" Julian said weakly in reply. For a moment Raedrick considered not doing it, but Julian would need to be able to at least move both his arms to make the trip back. Their eyes met and Julian rolled his, then gave a quick nod.

Raedrick pushed. Hard. Julian cried out, his eyes rolled back in their sockets, and he passed out.

<hr />

A couple minutes later, when Julian had come back to his senses, Raedrick helped him back into his clothing. It was slow going, with a lot of wincing and muttering on Julian's part, but at least he had some range of motion in the injured arm now. Once Julian was settled, Raedrick helped him to his feet.

Raedrick considered for a moment whether to bother with Julian's pack, then decided to just leave it. All of their meager remaining possessions fit easily into Raedrick's own pack, and he did not want to put any more weight onto Julian's shoulder than he had too. So instead, he took a moment to bury the pack under the snow. Then they set out to the south, Julian's arm over his shoulder as Raedrick supported him so he could walk.

Very quickly they lost the light entirely. Oh, there was some small amount of light from the stars overhead that filtered down through the canopy, but it was far from sufficient. And when - not if, but when - the clouds rolled through, that would be gone completely.

The memory of the drop-off that they almost ran into weighed heavily on Raedrick's mind as they walked. There were any number of hazards, many as bad or worse than that drop-off, that they could potentially meet here in the wild. And he could barely see his hands in front of his face.

Continuing on was madness. They needed to wait until light, or they both could die in some mishap that would be easily avoided during the day.

But he dared not stop. Geoff and his men were back there, not a mile distant. Skin-and-bones had to have reported back by now. Geoff would know he and Julian had escaped him, yet again.

Raedrick and Julian were well past a nuisance to Geoff. He almost had the prize in his hands, the thing he had lied, cheated, and killed to obtain. And Raedrick had cheated him of it. Or at least, that would be how Geoff saw it. Maybe losing yet another man, with two others wounded, would convince him to leave over, let them go, but Raedrick, regardless of what he had said to Julian earlier, rather doubted it. Geoff was the vindictive type; he did not let things go.

But there was vindictive anger and then there was sheer stupidity, and Geoff was not stupid. He would probably wait until it was light to set off after them again. And they could not be anywhere near the cave when that happened. They would be easy enough to track through the snow. No sense making it easier still.

And so they had no choice but to walk through the woods in the dark, on the side of a mountain.

At some point, Raedrick fell asleep.

He had no idea when, or how long he and Julian had stumbled along through the night. Hell, when sunlight on his face made him blink his eyes open, he for a moment did not remember that he was out in the wild, in the depths of winter, alone except for an injured friend, with a group of men bent of vengeance probably right on his heels. For a moment, all he thought was how pleasant the sunlight felt, and how its refraction through a nearby icicle really was something to behold.

He smiled, drew in a deep breath.

And remembered.

He sat upright with a start, frantically turning his head left and right as he sought to get his bearings. Where was he? And Julian. Where was Julian?

The answer to the first question was simple enough. He sat in the middle of a thicket, dense except off to the right, where the underbrush had been roughly broken aside. The trees and brambles on all sides were bare, their leaves long since fallen to the earth and buried by snow or, in the case of the evergreens, high enough above him that they did not impact his initial look around. And yet the snow was less here than elsewhere; a quick glance past the broken brambles to the world beyond showed that. And there was less wind than Raedrick remembered. Even bare branches can help with that, it seemed.

But how had he gotten here? He had no memory of finding this place, or of stopping at all. One moment he was trudging along, trying to ignore the deepening cold, the numerous aches of his body, the crushing fatigue threatening to flatten him with every step, and the danger that forced him to keep taking that next step. So what had happened?

And, again, where was Julian?

He could not have left Raedrick, gone on alone. He was in no condition to do such a thing. That just left a few possibilities, and they were all bad.

The sound of footsteps in the snow brought Raedrick's attention to the rear. He spun around, or rather tried to, but even the lesser snow within the thicket was enough to make turning slow and cumbersome. Apprehension combined with the familiar feeling of adrenalin surging through his body as he readied himself for a fight...

Looking haggard, weary, with bruises showing all over his face, Julian nevertheless managed a half-smile as he pushed aside a branch and stomped into the thicket. The smile slipped as he settled his weight onto his forward foot, becoming a wince as he struggled to hold back a groan. "Morning, Rae," he managed, through clenched teeth.

Raedrick sprang to his feet, relief fighting with concern as he went to help his friend. "Take it easy," he said. Julian accepted his help, allowing Raedrick to support him as he lowered himself down into a seated position. "What do you think you're doing?"

Julian coughed. Winced. Then held up his right hand. Raedrick had not noticed it earlier: he was holding a dead rabbit. "Getting you breakfast," he said, and grinned again, slightly.

Raedrick blinked in surprise.

He must have looked as baffled as he felt, because Julian barked out a laugh that ended abruptly in a spasm of coughing, followed by a very colorful oath. "Set a snare last night," he said, finally.

How's that? "Julian, we were... It was..." He paused, trying to make sense of what Julian had said. "What?"

Julian grinned again, but though he looked amused enough to laugh again, he managed to restrain himself. One coughing fit in as many minutes was sufficient, Raedrick presumed. "You got downright delusional last night. I thought *I* felt bad, but you..." He shook his head. "Half of what you said made no sense, and you kept changing direction. At some point, we blundered in here," he gestured at the thicket all around, "and you said something about a snare, then just passed out."

"So you set a snare."

Julian nodded.

"In the dark."

Another nod.

"In your condition."

Julian just looked at him with a long-suffering expression on his face.

"And the damn thing actually caught something?" This was the most ridiculous thing he had ever heard, and if he had not seen it with his own eyes... Raedrick sighed. "What time is it?"

Julian shrugged. "I make it about eight in the morning," he said, and began clearing some of the snow from the ground in front of him. Or trying to; he paused after moving a couple handfuls, wincing as his left hand moved quickly to his right shoulder.

Eight in the morning. They did not have much time then. Raedrick stood reluctantly, his knees popping from the sudden movement of limbs that had gone stiff from the night spent on the ground, in the bitter cold. He was surprised they had made it through at all.

"We don't have time to cook, Julian," he said. "Geoff and his men will..."

Julian snorted. "I think you were right last night. He's not stupid, and his men are probably just as tired as we are. They're done with us for now. Maybe forever."

Raedrick was not so sure. Geoff would not let what happened slide, not that easily. Of course, from the look on Julian's face he did not want to hear that right then. No matter, there were other reasons to move out. "Regardless, we need to get you to the Healers Circle."

Julian shrugged. Shallowly. "Sleep did me good. I'm right as rain."

Raedrick looked at him levelly.

Their eyes met for a moment, then Julian lowered his eyes. He nodded, then slowly, with obvious effort, stood. He kept the rabbit in his hand. "Fine. I'll cook it when we get back."

Raedrick chuckled. "Come on. We can't be far from the cabin."

Raedrick was right. Once they descended the rest of the way down the hillside, which they accomplished in about a quarter of a mile, they turned downriver. Maybe a half-mile further on, they approached the little curved spit of land that formed the northern edge of the cove near the cabin. Their tracks from the other day were easy to see.

He grinned and slapped Julian on the back - he had gone back to leaning on Raedrick for support after the first few minutes of walking. He was no where near as well-off as he had tried to claim in the thicket.

Julian grinned as well, but did not speak. His eyes said all that needed saying. Thank the Gods, now let's get in that boat and get out of here.

Raedrick found he concurred completely.

He made to retrace his earlier steps out to the canoe, but the breeze shifted, bringing the smell of woodsmoke to his nostrils. He stopped cold, casting about for the source of the smoke.

"Rae," Julian said, urgency in his tone. He pointed west, toward the woods along the riverbank where Povol's cabin lay.

A thin trail of smoke, growing thicker by the second, rose there. There could be no doubt what was burning.

"Son of a bitch," Raedrick said in unison with Julian, then they hurried toward the cabin.

32

ON ICE

By the time they pressed through the woods to the small clearing where the cabin lay, it was too late. The whole structure was ablaze, the heat intense enough that they could not come within thirty feet of the place that had sheltered them so well just a day ago. Smoke billowed from the blaze, and all around loud popping noises began issuing from the trees and undergrowth. Ice that had coated, and in some cases penetrated, limbs was melting or splitting, taking some of the limbs with it. It would not be long before the closest trees were free of snow entirely, and then…

"This whole part of the woods is going to go up," Julian said. He was holding a hand up, shielding his face and eyes from the blaze as he peered around at the trees, some practically right on top of the burning cabin.

Raedrick nodded. Julian was right, and there was not a damn thing they could do to stop it. Maybe if Melanie were there, she could use some bit of Magery to quench the flame, but short of that… Anger welled up within him, more like righteous fury. "Geoff did this," he said through clenched teeth.

Julian looked sidelong at him, and for a second Raedrick thought he would disagree. But instead he nodded.

They stood there for a long moment, just watching the fire consuming Povol's cabin. The flames' movement as they whipped about in a frenzy was mesmerizing, the heat, intense as it was, lulling. It would be so easy to just stay there and watch, then continue to watch as the trees on either side caught fire as well, and then...

A thought struck Raedrick, and he jerked out of the brief reverie. "The canoe!"

Julian blinked, then groaned. "That bastard better not have."

They turned as one and rushed back toward the river and the boat Raedrick had left in the ice the day before.

The cold hit with renewed fury after a dozen steps, seeming doubly eager to trample them underfoot after their brief respite in the heat of the blaze and playing counterpoint to the cold sliver of fear that run up Raedrick's spine. If Geoff had destroyed the canoe, or taken it, they were screwed. It was a long walk back through the wooded valley then over Tollard's Peak to the Glamorwood. And shortly the valley's forest would be aflame; that would not make for a pleasant hike. Between the cold without and its twin within, Raedrick went from sweating to shivering in moments, and it seemed he would freeze between one running step and the next.

They made it along the north side of the cove and out onto the ice, and that sliver of fear became a lance.

The canoe was still there, but it was not alone. Geoff and two of his men, skin-and-bones and a swarthy, burly fellow with a black beard long enough he had braided it, stood between Raedrick and Julian and the boat, weapons drawn.

Geoff's vicious grin appeared immediately as the friends stepped into view. "Thought we'd find you here," he said, pitching his voice so it would carry easily across the twenty feet or so between them. "Like what we've done with the place?" He gestured with his battleaxe past Raedrick's shoulder, toward the burning cabin.

"Have you gone mad?" Raedrick demanded. "The entire forest is going to go up! It'll cook the men you left back at your camp, and us too unless we get out of here." He presumed Geoff had left the wounded back at their camp and marched these fellows down during the night.

"My men'll be fine. As for the forest," he shrugged, "that's on you, Constable. Now." Geoff lowered his axe, resting its head on the ice, and he laid his hands atop the weapon's handle. "That was pretty clever last night with the chest. How about you give me what's mine, and save us all any more trouble and unpleasantness."

Raedrick looked aside at Julian, who wore a scowl that made thunderclouds look bright, then sighed. "Geoff, the chest was empty. Someone else beat us all to it."

Skin-and-bones snorted loudly. "That's rich," he said, dripping derision as though he had forgotten how easily he had been beaten the night before. Raedrick found himself regretting that he let the man go.

"Have it your way," Geoff said, then hefted his axe. It was large, far longer than the smaller battleaxes the heavy infantry companies in the Army used. Those had been designed to wield one-handed, allowing the use of a shield as well. Geoff's axe looked almost a third longer than Raedrick's sword. He did not relish the thought of going up against that weapon.

Geoff nodded to his men. "Kill his friend. The Constable's mine."

The thugs advanced.

Typical. Raedrick had almost begun to believe that just this once they were going to make it out of this without a showdown. He sighed as he drew his blade and sidestepped to the left, putting some distance between himself and Julian so they would not interfere with each others' movements.

Why, oh, why did there always have to be a showdown?

33

SHOWDOWN

The footing would be treacherous. Snow covered the ice, lessening the danger somewhat, but if he was not careful, a poorly-placed foot would send Raedrick sliding to the ground, or even out into the frigid water. As battlefields went, this was about the worst one Raedrick would have picked.

Of course, Geoff and his men would suffer the same peril. If anything, they possibly were at more of a disadvantage than Raedrick and Julian. The two moving toward Julian would have to be careful of how they attacked, to avoid striking their partner or sliding into his attack. Julian would have no such limitation.

Which was all well and good, but it was not Raedrick's immediate problem.

Geoff's axe, dual-bladed and heavier than Raedrick would have ever considered wielding, whipped through the air in smooth arcs as he advanced. They were flourishes, not attacks, but Geoff performed them with effortless aplomb that bespoke great strength, as well as an intimate familiarity with the weapon and how to employ it.

Raedrick had no such bond with the longsword in his hand.

He swallowed, backing up a couple steps to maintain a comfortable distance between himself and Geoff.

Off to the right, skin-and-bones reached striking range of Julian, cutting downward at his injured right shoulder, but Julian easily avoided the blow, ducking outside the arc of the sword's cut and getting to the thug's quarter before he could pull back from the attack. A boot to skin-and-bones' hip sent him sprawling in front of his bearded comrade, who had to leap to avoid tripping over him.

And then Raedrick had no more time to spare noticing the details of Julian's fight. Geoff snarled, a ravenous light in his eyes, and lunged forward, the great axe cutting toward Raedrick's belly.

The straightforward attack caught Raedrick by surprise; he had expected something more...elegant. But while the attack was not fancy, it was effective, and Raedrick was almost too slow in his defense. He brought his longsword down in a descending arc intended to knock Geoff's blade aside and set himself up for a riposte.

And found that the great axe was no longer there.

Oh, it was still present, but it no longer veered toward Raedrick's gut, but instead whipped upward toward his throat.

Raedrick spat out a curse and hopped backward, tilting his head backwards and whispering a quick prayer in his mind; there was nothing else he could do, the feint had tricked him so.

The axe's passing came with its own gentle breeze, and then it was gone as Geoff recovered from his swing and pulled back to a guarding position. Raedrick thought the cut had missed for a second, then he felt the ache starting. He raised his left hand to his chin, and his glove came away bloody.

Geoff smirked and spun the great axe in his hands. A few drops of blood splattered onto the snow-covered ice between them. "I reckon I'm going to enjoy this," he said.

Julian grimaced as he brought his sword up. His shoulder still throbbed, despite Raedrick's first aid the night before, and his arm did not move as well as it normally did. He was barely able to get the parry up in time to meet the incoming attack.

Steel met steel and the two blades rang as one for a moment. The attack had been a clumsy back-handed swing, the best braid-beard could do with his balance off after leaping over his fallen comrade. But he managed to put a fair amount of force behind the cut, and Julian's arm buckled, bending involuntarily at the elbow and allowing the encroaching steel to come mere inches from his neck.

Braid-beard grinned and pressed his advantage, throwing his weight against his sword.

Julian laid his left hand overtop his right on the grip of his blade, trying to reinforce his failing arm, but slowly, surely, he was losing it. The angle was wrong and the brigand had all the leverage. Any second now, Julian's sword arm would give way altogether, and then he was done.

"Time's up," Braid-beard taunted. He pressed forward even harder.

Julian relaxed his sword arm and twisted, letting the force of the brigand's shove turn his body clockwise and backward. Julian gave one last shove against the brigand's blade as he twisted, not opposing his force but redirecting it, and then his body was out of the way of the attack. Spinning completely around, he returned the braid-beard's backhanded cut with one of this own.

Braid-beard moved forward with the momentum of his push, then staggered as Julian suddenly was no longer there. Julian's sword swept through next as he completed his spin, and Julian felt the telltale resistance of the steel cutting into the brigand's flesh above the hip.

Braid-beard lurched forward, stumbling as the wound began to register. His left hand went to his hip, where blood had begun to flow, and a confused expression came over his face. He made as if to take a step. And then his leg buckled and he fell in a heap into the snow. His sword landed, uselessly, next to him. Only then did he cry out, a long loan moan of pain that sounded as though it came through gritted teeth.

Julian rose to his full height and nodded in satisfaction. One down.

He turned back toward the other brigand, and his satisfaction faded quickly. The scrawny fellow was back on his feet, moving toward Julian with much greater deliberation than he had at first. Scrawny's eyes flickered between Julian and his fallen comrade, and he licked his lips, from nerves hopefully.

Julian stepped back, giving himself some distance from the fallen man, and made to lift his sword to a guarding position.

His right arm would not move.

Or at least, it would not move past about twenty degrees from pointing straight down. This was not good, not at all.

Scrawny saw his difficulty and any nervousness faded. He grinned hungrily and advanced.

The cut was bleeding badly; it must have been pretty deep. But Raedrick's chin merely ached; it did not burn with the pain that such blood flow would seem to dictate. He had suffered deep wounds before, so he was pretty sure he knew the difference.

Time to worry about that later.

Geoff advanced again, his too-long axe spinning a circle that reflected the sunlight, causing Raedrick to blink for a second. Only instinct and a desperate dive to the side prevented him from being chopped in half by the attack that followed.

Raedrick rolled over his left shoulder and sprang to his feet, only to see the cutting edge of Geoff's weapon descending toward his head. Moving with a speed born of desperation, he side-stepped to the left and flicked his sword right. Steel met steel with a sharp clang, and Geoff's axe rebounded from Raedrick's sword, continuing its descent past Raedrick's right shoulder. Raedrick kept moving, sidestepping further to his left and flicking the cutting edge of his sword toward Geoff's right shoulder.

Geoff began moving as soon as the parry deflected his cut, drawing his right leg back and twisting his body out of the way of Raedrick's counter. It was almost as though he knew what Raedrick was going to do before he did it, he moved so smoothly.

Raedrick retreated a step, drawing a deep breath and raising his blade back to vertical in front of himself. His heart pounded in his ears from the exertion of the duel, and his entire body felt as though it were going to fly apart, he was charged up so.

Geoff paused and, frowning slightly, removed his left hand from the grip of his axe. He raised it to his right shoulder, and the fingertips came away red. Geoff sniffed and raised his eyebrows at Raedrick.

Raedrick glanced quickly at the end of his sword. The tip - the very tip - was lightly stained with blood. A small drop pooled and began running down the blood groove in the middle of the blade. So his cut had not been completely ineffectual after all.

He had not realized how much the speed and efficacy of Geoff's initial attacks had put a damper on his spirits. But seeing his opponent's blood on his blade - however little - the confidence Raedrick had not realized was fading rebounded within him. He returned Geoff's raised eyebrows with a quick grin - *that* hurt a *lot* - and rolled his shoulders, settling down into a more relaxed ready stance.

Then it was his turn to advance.

He darted forward and to the right, thrusting straight ahead with his sword ever so briefly before cutting straight down at Geoff's left thigh.

Again the thug moved as though reading Raedrick's mind. He did not even try to deflect the feint; he merely hopped backwards a half-step, allowing Raedrick's cut to pass harmlessly through the air where his leg used to be.

Then he countered with a sweeping cut at neck-level.

Gotcha.

Raedrick stopped his rightward movement and, crouching low, slid his left leg far out to the side and shifted his weight onto it. Geoff's decapitation strike whistled harmlessly through the air over his head, close enough that his hair billowed softly in the breeze of its passing. Raedrick countered immediately with an upward cut, angling to the left so that it would open Geoff up from left hip to right shoulder.

Again the thug was not quite quick enough. He moved out of each of Raedrick's sword, but not before Raedrick scored a cut on his hip.

The big man stumbled as he retreated and the pain of the new wound registered, but he regained his balance quickly. Again his left hand left his axe's grip and went to the wound, but this time it was no mere scratch; the blood began flowing immediately, staining his furs with a quickly-growing circle of red.

"You're right, Geoff," Raedrick said in his most derisive tone. "This is fun."

Geoff's nostrils flared and he barked out a curse. Then, the pain of his new wound apparently forgotten, he launched himself forward.

Julian backpedalled, ducking beneath a high cut, and countered. But though he had trained to fight left-handed - that was simply a prudent thing for a fighting man to do - his swing felt almost as awkward as it looked, and Scrawny sidestepped it easily.

This was not going well at all.

The brigand wasted no time, but instead pressed forward with his own attack. A smile wrought from the assurance of victory bespoke the man's outlook on the fight more than any boast could have. He was going to win out, and soon. Trouble was, Julian tended to agree with him.

He half-stepped, half-slid to the side and sucked in his gut, just barely getting his belly out of the way of Scrawny's sword.

For a second, the brigand was wide open for a counter attack from above, but Julian's sword was out of position still. And he did not feel confident in pressing the attack. So instead he retreated.

Several quick shuffle-steps backward put about ten feet between himself and Scrawny, and Julian paused to take his bearings.

Off to his right, Raedrick still had his hands full with Geoff. The two men danced around each other, Raedrick barely avoiding being gutted by that extra-long axe twice in as many seconds. To the left, the nearly frozen river flowed through the channel it had cut in the ice. That channel was close now, just a dozen feet away. To the front, past Scrawny, the smoke from the cabin fire still rose from beyond the little rocky cove. And more; the smoke column was wider, thicker. The trees must have caught fire.

Julian's opponent rolled his shoulders, the movement drawing Julian's attention back to the brigand, who grinned again and advanced, more quickly this time.

Probably wants to get this over with in a hurry.

Bloody fool.

The attack was simple, a thrust straight toward Julian's navel. He made a show of failing to parry it and hopped backward instead, giving ground again to avoid the attack. Then he countered with a backhanded cut toward Scrawny's neck. It was far from steady, but it was the best cut he could manage right then.

Once again, the brigand avoided it easily, simply batting it aside with a nearly contemptuous parry before shuffling forward again, this time cutting straight down toward Julian's uninjured left shoulder.

Julian pivoted on his right foot, spinning out of the way of the descending blade and drawing his body perpendicular to his attacker - a fine stance to minimize the target area he presented, except that it placed his injured shoulder, and not his sword, closest to Scrawny.

The thug could not fail to take advantage of that opening, so

Julian did not give him the chance to. Quickly shifting his weight onto his left foot, he snapped the edge of his right foot out.

The sole of Julian's boot met the side of Scrawny's left knee with a dull popping sound. Scrawny's eyes widened in sudden pain and shock, and he stumbled and fell, the leg giving out completely beneath him.

The brigand hit the ice, his sword, forgotten, clattering down beside him as he clutched both hands against his injured knee and let out a high-pitched shriek of pain.

Julian let his own sword fall to the ice and, gritting his teeth through the pain, forced his right arm to move. Squatting down and grabbing the thug's right boot with both hands, he growled something even he could not understand at the man, then forced his legs straight and spun his body around, clockwise.

The pain in his shoulder flared, and spots of light appeared in Julian's vision. He gritted his teeth and a new pain lanced out as he bit down on his tongue, but he forced himself to continued pulling Scrawny along.

The snow layer atop the ice was thinner here, near to the flowing water, and it proved little impediment to the momentum Julian managed to build up. Scrawny spun slowly at first, but very quickly he was moving at a good clip in a circle centered on Julian's body. He cried out again, in surprise as much as pain Julian presumed, and released his injured knee, reaching up toward Julian's hands where they gripped his ankle.

Julian released the boot.

Scrawny slid across the ice toward the flowing water, only a few feet away. The hapless man recognized immediately what was happening, and he clawed desperately at the ice to slow his progress.

But it was too little too late. With a cry even more shrill than the one he had made when Julian broke his knee, the man reached the edge of the ice and went over.

He came up briefly, his hands, shaking horribly even after such a short immersion, grasping at the ice's edge. He croaked out a feeble, "Help me!" And then he lost his grip and submerged fully.

He did not bob up to the surface again.

Julian, out of breath from his exertion, fell to his knees and inhaled deeply. Relief flooded through him, almost enough to eclipse the pain of his shoulder. Almost. He raised a trembling left hand to the injured joint and probed it, and the pain increased immediately.

"Damn it," he muttered.

A cry of pain from behind drew him from his inward focus, and Julian turned to see Raedrick stumbling backwards away from Geoff. The thug's battleaxe was stained red; a particularly nasty cut on Raedrick's left shoulder stood out in Julian's view.

He needed help. Now.

"Always the hero," Julian muttered to himself. Then he picked up his sword in his left hand and forced himself to his feet. The change in posture caused more pain to shoot from his shoulder for a moment, and he tasted blood. He spat red; he must have done his tongue really well.

Then, hefting his sword in his bad hand, he trudged forward as quickly as he could.

The pain in his left shoulder eclipsed his other wounds as Raedrick retreated quickly. It was all he could do not to fall over as he scrambled away, barely avoiding yet another cut from Geoff's great axe.

He had thought he was getting the upper hand after scoring that last cut on the burly man, but if anything it only seemed to infuriate Geoff all the more. He came at Raedrick in a blazing whir of steel that almost overwhelmed him completely. It was only through sheer luck that he had only escaped with the cut on his shoulder.

But it could not last. He had no illusions there. Soon, quite soon, he would falter and Geoff would take him.

He tried a counter attack, but Geoff merely attacked in kind and the longer reach of the thug's weapon forced Raedrick to abandon his cut and dive to the side to avoid being eviscerated. He came up in a roll, facing Geoff, and brought his sword up between them.

The thug grinned, again. "You're done, Constable. Might as well save us both the trouble and admit it."

Raedrick swallowed hard and returned the grin with the hardest glare he could muster, then he spat at the thug's feet.

Geoff's grin widened and he advanced again.

Raedrick ducked beneath the shoulder-level cut and surged forward, lowering his shoulder toward Geoff's injured hip. If he could just get him off balance…

Geoff became a blur of motion and something struck Raedrick in the side. Hard. He went reeling, and almost passed out from the pain as he landed hard on his injured arm. He let out a groan and flipped himself onto his back. Then he found he could move no more, and he just lay there, looking up at the morning clouds wafting across the sky.

Geoff's face abruptly blotted them out. He looked down at Raedrick in silence for a moment, then he shook his head and raised his axe. "Bye, Constable."

The axe began to fall.

It moved in slow motion. Raedrick could not take his eyes away from it. Somewhere in his brain, Raedrick shouted at himself to evade, to get his own blade up to parry. Something. But he could not force himself into motion.

This was it; the end.

Then Geoff's face went slack and his eyes rolled back in their sockets. The great axe, which had begun the killing blow, faltered, then fell from Geoff's suddenly limp hands and clattered to the ice harmlessly.

Geoff fell like a sack of potatoes, landing with a solid thump on the ice next to Raedrick.

A moment later, Julian looked down at him from where Geoff had been. He shook his head with a sardonic grin. "I'm *always* pulling your chestnuts out of the fire, Rae." Then, chuckling, he gingerly wiped his sword clean, slid into his belt, and held his left hand down to Raedrick.

Raedrick accepted the hand up and could not help laughing himself. Right then it seemed very appropriate.

❦ 34 ❦

HOMEBOUND

"You look like hell, Rae. Gonna be one nasty scar."

Raedrick wanted to scowl, but that would just make his chin hurt worse. Turns out that first cut had sliced clean through to the bone, leaving a flap of his skin dangling from his chin. It had taken Julian a long time to get that bandaged up, wrapping his head in what felt like miles of cloth.

Raedrick grunted and replied, "Can't be helped." He pulled the knot he was tying snug and straightened, checking his handiwork.

Geoff lay on the ice before him, tied hand and foot with strips of cloth they had torn from the thug's cloak, a bruise on his left temple that seemed to grow larger and darker by the second. He breathed shallowly, actually snoring softly as he lay there.

Raedrick shook his head and glanced aside at Julian. "You hit him hard enough. Lucky he's not dead."

Julian shrugged noncommittally. "Meant him to be. Next time I'll try harder."

Raedrick snorted. "Then why didn't you just run him through?"

Julian shrugged again but did not respond otherwise.

Raedrick grinned, not pushing the issue. Let Julian keep up the hard act if he wanted to; he was honorable and respected the law as much as Raedrick did. More maybe. And he wanted to see Geoff publicly tried and punished too. A violent death out in the wild might have been acceptable if the conditions warranted it, but stabbing the man in the back? Raedrick had never seen Julian come close to doing that, even while protecting another. He had always found a way to at least make it sporting.

"Let's get him to the boat."

Julan sighed, but he nodded and bent over, grabbing hold of the bindings around Geoff's ankles with his good arm. The other hung in a sling that Raedrick had fashioned from the rest of Geoff's cloak after they had bandaged their various wounds - and Geoff's - with it. Julian must have cut the other thug deeper than he thought; by the time they had come around to him, he had already bled out. Which was just as well, as they had about ran out of cloth for bandages, anyway, after binding their own wounds.

Raedrick grabbed Geoff by the shoulders and they lifted together.

Gods, was he heavy! It took a seeming eternity to move him the few tens of feet to the boat. They had to stop several times to rest, and even with that it was almost too much for them. Getting him situated in the canoe, in the center between the two bench-seats forward and in the rear, and then tying him in place was almost as difficult as the carrying; twice they almost capsized the boat in the struggle. But eventually they managed it.

They paused for a long minute, breathing heavily from the exertion.

"Guess it's too late to change your mind about this," Julian said, but his tone was teasing; he did not mean it. Or at least he knew Raedrick's mind was set.

Raedrick nodded.

"Best get to it then."

Raedrick chuckled and cuffed Julian lightly on his good shoulder. "Thought you'd never ask."

With that, they settled into the canoe, Julian in the front - with his injured shoulder he could hardly paddle, let alone steer - and Raedrick in the rear. They shoved off and very quickly, the current carried them away downstream toward Lake Glimmermere.

Gods willing, it would be a smooth ride, and then an easy hike, all the way home.

❊ 35 ❊

WRAPPING UP

G eoff glared at Raedrick from behind the bars of his cell, the scowl on his face enough to knock a deer over at fifty paces. "You'll pay for this, Constable. Mark me."

The cell was the center in a set of three similar units that ran the length of the corridor behind Raedrick and Julian's office in the Constabulary. Opposite them, three more cells of identical make stood empty. For that matter, the other two on Geoff's side were devoid of occupants as well. Few in Lydelton actually caused trouble, and most of those who did were just men who had consumed too much at the Oarlock or Holb's; after they slept it off they were generally all right to set loose, minus the fine the judge always demanded of course.

The last time more than one of the cells had been used for any length of time had been in the aftermath of the battle with Isenholf's brigands, when Raedrick and Julian first came to Glimmer Vale almost a year ago. The surviving brigands, and Isenholf himself, had packed the cells full for a couple weeks while awaiting the Judge. With that crisis long in the past, Raedrick did not expect to ever fill them all again, not from the town's inhabitants anyway.

It had been more difficult getting back to town than it should have been, with Geoff in tow, but it could have been worse. He had awoken a half hour after they got underway in the canoe and promptly set about trying to upset the boat. A whack over the head with Julian's paddle - light enough to not actually hurt him but hard enough to leave an impression - and a stern reminder that he would go in with them and he hadn't even a prayer of swimming to safety tied as he was put a stop to that quickly.

When they reached the solid ice of Lake Glimmermere they had a hell of a time getting him out of the boat and onto his feet. But eventually, they convinced him it was follow along with them or die right then and there, so he went along, if not willingly, then with little enough fuss.

They took Tolburt's route: straight across the ice toward the town. It was more direct, flatter, and promised a quicker trip than going to the shore. The ice was certainly thick enough to hold them all - Raedrick reminded himself of that every dozen paces or so - so the decision was easy to make.

They made it to town shortly after sunset, moving on stiff legs against a bitter breeze that blew in from the east. Raedrick had wanted nothing more than to throw Geoff into a cell and go home for a long night's sleep.

But there were other matters to attend to, and he spent a while after getting Geoff situated checking on Ravi and Povol. The latter was under the Guildsman's care in the Healers Circle. For his part, Ravi had developed a cough at some point. Every couple minutes the old man had to pause to hack forcefully, but when Raedrick asked about it, he waved it off as nothing of import. Povol was the greater concern. And he was; his hand looked even worse than Raedrick remembered, despite Ravi's treatments. The Guildsman suspected he would lose at least one finger.

Luckily, Povol was not awake to hear that.

Ravi insisted that Raedrick and Julian remain at the Circle long enough to properly dress their wounds before they turned in for the night. It took a dozen stitches to close up the cut on Raedrick's chin and half again as many for his shoulder, but sick as he was,

Ravi managed it so deftly that Raedrick hardly felt the pricks of the needle. Julian was not so lucky when Ravi re-set his shoulder. He howled even worse than he had when Raedrick set it out in the wilderness. Ravi extracted a reluctant promise from Julian to return first thing in the morning for a check-up, and then they were done.

Raedrick finally walked - more like staggered - to the little flat he called home. He did not even manage to remove his boots before he fell onto his bed, exhausted, and slept until the long hours of the morning.

When he awoke, all he wanted to do was pull his blankets over his head and go back to sleep, but his responsibilities forced their way into his mind and would not shut up. So, reluctantly, he got up and, pausing only to change into fresh clothes, he headed back to the office, and his prisoner.

And so his first conversation of the day began with Geoff's surly words of warning.

Raedrick raised an eyebrow at Geoff's comment, then gave the cell door a tug. It rattled in place, but did not move. "Perhaps," he said, "but not today."

Geoff opened his mouth to respond but Raedrick kept right on rolling.

"Nor tomorrow, I expect. Tomorrow you go before the judge, and I don't think he'll take kindly to your activities here. Confidence games," he raised one finger, "assault," another, "attempting murder," a third, "vandalism," a fourth, "theft," his thumb, "kidnapping." Raedrick shook his head and whistled ever so softly.

Geoff shut his mouth, his scowl growing darker.

"Breakfast will be here in a few minutes," Raedrick said, turning away from the cell and its occupant.

In fact, the food arrived almost as soon as he returned to the front office, shut the door to the cell block, and settled into the chair behind his desk. The door cracked open, admitting the wind, which was cold and energetic this morning and threatened to overwhelm the heat the stove in the corner put out. The delivery man from The Oarlock, clad in a thick coat, matching leggings, and a cowled cloak, shut the door quickly and stamped his boots to clear them of snow, then pushed back his hood.

Raedrick blinked. *Her* hood. Or more in particular, Lani's hood. He rose to his feet in a rush, smiling in greeting. "Lani," he began.

She silenced him with a look that put the wind to shame in its chill and set a small satchel, containing Geoff's and his breakfast no doubt, onto his desk. "Your order, Constable," she said in a level businesslike tone that would seem perfectly professional to someone who did not know her.

What was going on here?

"Thank you," he said. "It's good to see you."

She snorted, then turned and headed toward the door, his shoulders set in the posture Raedrick had seen her use a time or two, when she was furious.

"What - ?"

She stopped at his question, her hand partly raised to the door latch. She stood there for a few seconds, then she drew in a quick breath that almost sounded like a sob. "I was so worried," she said. "When you didn't return after two days, I knew something horrible had happened. And then when Master Sebastini and Povol got back..." She shook her head, still not looking at him. She sniffled, and Raedrick knew she was crying.

He stepped around the desk to go to her, but she whirled around, raising her hand, palm out toward him in a stopping gesture. Tears ran down her cheeks and her lips trembled, but her eyes burned with fury - she was probably at least as angry that she had lost her composure as anything else, if he had to make a guess.

"And then this morning I find out that you returned last night. I found out from a *messenger*." She drew a deep breath, wiping her eyes with the back of her glove. "We were open until two o'clock last night. You did not bother to come tell me yourself?"

Taken aback, Raedrick did not know how to respond for a second. He had been so tired last night, he had not even thought...

He had not even thought.

He hung his head, shame flooding through him as he realized what he had put her through while he was so absorbed in his own issues. "I'm sorry."

She looked at him, at his bandaged wounds, and tears welled up. "I told you I could not bear it if anything happened to you, and look..." She gestured toward his face and her voice caught. Her fingers curled into a fist that she raised before her mouth, to cover the beginnings of a sob.

Before he could say another word, she turned, opened the door, and left. The cold wind that entered the room with her passage seemed fitting, just then. It matched the ache in his chest.

He started toward the door, intending to follow her, to explain. But he held short before he had covered half the distance. What was there to say? He had his responsibilities, and he had put them before her. Hell, he had put them before everything - before his own safety, that of his friends. She was right to be angry with him. He would find a way to make amends, but it seemed clear she did not want to hear about it just then.

Sighing, he turned away from the door and picked up the satchel of foodstuffs, but paused as he heard through the door leading back into the cell block - just a collection of wrought iron bars, like the doors to the cells - Geoff's mocking laughter.

✤ 36 ✤

PENANCE

"I'm such a fool." Tolburt hung his head, refusing to look up at Raedrick, or even at anything except his own lap. After a second, his breath caught and it sounded as though he was weeping, or trying very hard to keep from doing so.

They sat in the treatment room at the Healers Circle, and Raedrick had just finished telling the events of the last several days. He tried to keep a stern, calm face while doing the telling. But especially now, as Tolburt broke down, he had to work hard to maintain his bearing, so he thought of other things to keep himself calm: the sound of wind through the trees, the taste of finely mulled wine on a crisp autumn day, the pleasant ache of his muscles after a hard workout in the sparring ring with Julian.

Finally, Tolburt got himself a bit more under control. He wiped his nose on the back of his left hand and glanced quickly up at Raedrick. "How could I have not seen Stefan was playing me?"

Raedrick shrugged, but said nothing. This was the sort of thing Tolburt was going to have to figure out himself. It was well past time he grew up, truly grew up.

Tolburt must have seen the disapproval - the disappointment - in Raedrick's gaze because he lowered his eyes again. "Thank you for..."

"Do not thank me."

Tolburt recoiled at the rebuke in Raedrick's tone. He had used his best dressing-down voice; that had always worked wonders with subordinates who stepped out of line, and now with subjects of his - infrequent - investigations around town.

"You caused a lot of trouble for my town, Tolburt. Julian will be a long time recovering from his injuries. His shoulder may not ever be the same again. Povol lost two fingers, all of his dogs, and his dogsleds. Master Sebastini developed a bad cough, and at his age..." Raedrick trailed off, letting the rest go unsaid. He prayed Ravi did not take a turn for the worse. He was a gem of a man, and almost more important than that, the town could ill afford to lose its Guildsman in the middle of the winter. He drew a breath, putting that worry from his mind as he continued on. "And then there's the destroyed cabin and the forest fire. You have a lot to answer for."

"Me? But I..."

"Yes, you. Oh you were led astray, conned by Geoff's man." Raedrick jabbed a finger at Tolburt and he sank even further back into his pillows than he had already. "But you should have known enough to see through it. Instead you went willingly to be fleeced, and then you dragged us into it as well."

Tolburt's mouth opened and shut wordlessly for half a minute as he struggled to find some way to reply. His expression said he could not believe what Raedrick was saying, that he was being wronged. After everything that had happened, that was what angered Raedrick the most. He really did not see how he was responsible. Well, he would have time to figure it out.

"I've spoken with the Mayor and the Judge, and this is what's going to happen."

Tolburt went pale. Good.

"You will stay here and get well. When you're better, you'll check into a room at Bigsbe's Boarding House. You'll work at Holb's Tavern until the thaw, doing anything and everything he tells you without complaint. Your pay will go toward the supplies to rebuild the cabin and toward replacing Povol's sled dogs. After the thaw, you'll help Povol and the other men who owned that cabin rebuild."

Tolburt's mouth dropped open wide. He looked speechlessly at Raedrick, his eyes unbelieving.

"When everything that's happened has been put right, I'll give you the note we found in the chest. You can leave the Vale, follow the note to wherever it leads, whatever. But not before." Raedrick stood from his chair and took a step to the edge of Tolburt's bed. He was looming, and it was working. "Do you understand?"

Tolburt nodded silently.

"Good." Raedrick managed a half-smile that he hoped was at least a little comforting. "Welcome to Glimmer Vale, Tolburt. If you play your cards right while you're here, you may find you've finally become a man." He held Tolburt's gaze for a moment, then nodded briskly and turned away.

When he pulled the door shut behind him, Tolburt still had not said a word.

Raedrick met Julian down at the docks, as they had planned before Tolburt came to town and threw things out of kilter. He trudged through the snow past the Covington Brothers' warehouse, his head down and his hands shoved into the deep pockets of his coat in anticipation of the bitter wind that blew in off the lake. But for whatever reason the breeze was still this afternoon, and when Raedrick stopped in front of Julian, one of his eyebrows drifted upward in droll amusement. Or at least Raedrick presumed it was amusement; the rest of his face was covered by a thick red, yellow, and brown scarf so it was impossible to tell. But Julian being Julian…

"I believe the world is about to end, Rae." He gestured around at the lack of wind.

Raedrick nodded. "Surely that scarf is one of the prophesied precursors."

Julian snorted, or maybe laughed briefly. "A gift from Molli." He stamped his feet as though unwilling to stay still for too long lest the cold overcome him. Not a bad thought, actually. "Lani still mad?"

Raedrick nodded again. "We talked again last night, but..." But he was going to be in trouble for a while over this one.

Julian sighed, and the tone of the sigh carried worlds of commiseration. For a second Raedrick thought he was about to offer some manner of advice or other. Instead, he simply said, "We going to do this?"

"Aye," Raedrick replied. The situation with Lani could wait. Raedrick forced down a resigned sigh, then turned and led the way past the first two docks.

At the stairs leading up to Dock One, a familiar older man with thick grey hair to his shoulders and a beard of nearly the same length stood waiting for them. As always, he wore his battered old wool cloak. The only other concession he made to the bitter cold was the furred clothing he wore below the cloak; he did not even wear a hat. Years - hell, decades - of work out on the fishing boats had hardened him against the ravages of the elements, or at least that was what he wanted others to think.

The old fishing man looked the two of them over as they approached and inclined his head in greeting. "Constables. My boys got things set up as you asked."

"Thank you, Horace."

Horace shrugged. "No skin off my back. Can't see why you'd want to do this, but it's your funeral."

Raedrick tried to grin in response to the teasing tone the old fishing man took at the end, but the stitches in his chin warned him against it. Instead he just nodded then mounted the steps to the dock.

Julian remained behind for a moment, exchanging a few low words with Horace. The two had made fast friends when Julian and Raedrick first came to town, and Julian almost never passed up a chance to exchange words - and usually more than enough drink - with the old man.

Raedrick did not wait, but continued down the dock toward the end, where a small table had been laid out, along with two chairs. As he had asked, a single bottle lay uncorked on the table, and three glasses were set out, waiting for them. Just as it had been this time last year - well, almost as it had been anyway. It was far more cold here than it had been on the tropical docks of Qoramyr, and, of course Lydelton had no taverns on the docks themselves. But he and Julian had promised each other to do it like they had every year, and this was the best they could do.

"I told you before," Julian said from behind him. "We can do this just as well indoors."

Raedrick gave him a level look and settled down into the east-facing chair so he could watch the approaching sunset. "No we can't. This is our penance, Julian." He picked up the bottle - good whiskey all the way form Tol Guldor, very hard to come by - and poured two fingers' worth into the three glasses. "Part of it," he added softly, not meaning for the words to reach Julian's ears.

Julian sat opposite him and tugged the scarf down from his mouth. That eyebrow raised again. "Penance?" He shook his head disdainfully.

He did not understand, but Raedrick did not expect him to. Julian felt the loss of their comrades, and maybe felt a tinge of conscience over their desertion - their treason. But if he did, he never showed it; in fact he had tried on more than one occasion to set Raedrick's mind more fully at ease over the whole thing. They had done the right thing. To stay would have been the true betrayal, of all the principles they had sworn to uphold when they joined the Army. Of the reasons the war had begun in the first place.

And he was right. But he was also wrong. He had the luxury of only focusing on that part of the picture, but he had not been in command. In the end, it was Raedrick's decision that set them on the course that had resulted in so many of his men's deaths - and of Tolburt's fall. It had been the right thing to do, but the cost...

He took hold of his glass and raised it high between them. Julian followed suit.

"To our lost brothers, and those who cannot be with us."

Julian clinked his glass against Raedrick's. "One too few lost," he murmured softly before throwing the whiskey back in one smooth swallow.

Raedrick froze for a heartbeat. That comment could only refer to Tolburt. He knew Julian disapproved of allowing him to remain in town any longer than it took for him to recover fully. Patch him up and send him off, he had said. In truth, Raedrick had been tempted to do just that, except it would have been tantamount to an execution; there was no way Tolburt could make it through the passes before thaw, not alone. And there would be no caravans for months yet, if at all. And there was the possibility that this could help Tolburt finally get himself squared away.

But that was not the only reason. Raedrick had re-read the cryptic note they found within that chest half a dozen times. Something about it tweaked at his memory, but he could not lay his finger on what. It piqued his curiosity. Having a few more months to ponder its meaning would not be a bad thing.

Raedrick let Julian's words pass unanswered, instead downing his own whiskey just a hair slower than Julian had.

Julian smirked; he was no fool. But he said no more, just picked up the third glass and flung its contents over the railing of the dock and onto the frozen lake.

They sat there for a time, trading tales of their lost comrades and sharing drinks, just the three of them - Raedrick, Julian, and the ghost of the past. Finally, the bottle empty, the two men stood and stumbled back to the shore, leaning against each other for support against the swimming of their heads.

And somewhere during all of that, Raedrick realized the other side of his decision of two years ago. It had resulted in tragedy for too many of his men. But some of them had found new lives, and he and Julian made it here, to this place. There was a lot of good here, a lot of good people, and they were helping to make it better. They had built a home, a place where they could do some good and turn away from their past. And maybe that was enough. If nothing else, it was a good start.

They left the dock and went their separate ways, Julian grumbling about needing to turn in early because of an early appointment with Ravi. Raedrick watched him go and could not help but laugh at the drunken annoyance in his friend's tone. Then he turned on unsteady legs and headed toward The Oarlock. Lani was working again tonight, and he found he was no longer content to let their reconciliation happen on its own schedule.

He set as strong a pace as he could muster without tripping over himself. On the way there, he passed several townsfolk who were trudging through the streets on business of one sort or other. Each and every one of them looked at him askance, and it was not until he turned into The Oarlock's stable yard that he realized why.

He had been whistling the whole way there.

Raedrick placed his hand on The Oarlock's front door and managed a smile despite the lingering pain of the cut to his chin. Yes, this was a good place. And if he had anything to say in the matter, it would remain so for a good long time.

Squaring his shoulders, he pushed the door open and stepped inside, out of the cold.

MESSAGE FROM THE AUTHOR

Thank you for reading my book. I hope you enjoyed reading it as much as I enjoyed writing it.

Every review helps an author out, so whether you loved this book, hated it, or something in between, please take a minute to tell other readers what you thought. All of the online retailers make it very easy to do, and I would really appreciate it.

Feel free to come say hi at my website or on Gab. I always enjoy hearing from readers, especially since you all are, collectively, my boss.

I also have a weekly podcast, Story Time With Michael Kingswood, where I read stories and talk through some of the latest goings on in my world. I'd love to see you there.

Thanks again. My best to you and yours.

Warm Regards,
Michael Kingswood

MAILING LIST

If you enjoyed this book and would like word on new releases and special deals from Michael Kingswood, sign up for his newsletter on his website. Guaranteed to be spam-free, you can opt out at any time. And you can rest assured he will not share your information with anyone, for any reason.

https://michaelkingswood.com/newsletter-signup/

MEMBERSHIP

Michael would like to invite you to become a supporting member of his website. Similar in concept to Patreon, a few dollars a month will give you access to exclusive content, and help him to focus more of his time to writing fun and exciting stories for your enjoyment.

Sign up at his website:

https://www.michaelkingswood.com/membership/join/

ABOUT THE AUTHOR

Michael Kingswood is 20-year veteran of the US Navy submarine force and a lifelong fan of science fiction and fantasy literature. His work has appeared in numerous collections and anthologies, to include the Fiction River Anthology series from WMG publishing. He holds a bachelors degree in Mechanical Engineering as well as a Master of Engineering Management and a Master of Business Administration. He has four children and currently resides in San Diego.

Find Michael Kingswood online at:

www.michaelkingswood.com

www.facebook.com/michael.kingswood

twitter.com/michaelkingswd

MORE BOOKS BY MICHAEL KINGSWOOD

GLIMMER VALE CHRONICLES

Glimmer Vale

Out-Dweller

Tollard's Peak

Robbed Blind

The Falconer's Stairs

Glimmer Vale Omnibus Edition #1

STORIES FROM GLIMMER VALE

Legacy

Hidden Magic

Captive Hearts

Wedding Gifts

Lost Credit

THE PERICLES CONSPIRACY

Passing In The Night

The Pericles Conspiracy

DAWN OF ENLIGHTENMENT

Masters Of The Sun

NOVELLAS

What Lurks Between

The Necromancer's Lair

The Champion

Veritas Morte

STORY COLLECTIONS

Stories From The Great Challenge

Tales Of Adventure #1

Tales Of Adventure #2

Short Story 10-Pack

A Jar Of Mixed Treats

Short Mystery 10-Pack

Stories From Glimmer Vale, Volume 1

SHORT FICTION

Michael has also published a number of shorter works, links to which can
be found on his website.